Incredible Dreams?

Incredible Dreams?

Robert E. Bonson

*To: Ian
Enjoy
Bob
6/03*

Copyright © 2001 by Robert E. Bonson.

Library of Congress Number: 2001118678
ISBN #:   Softcover   1-4010-2983-3

All rights reserved. No part of this book may be reproduced or transmitted in any form or by any means, electronic or mechanical, including photocopying, recording, or by any information storage and retrieval system, without permission in writing from the copyright owner.

This is a work of fiction. Names, characters, places and incidents either are the product of the author's imagination or are used fictitiously, and any resemblance to any actual persons, living or dead, events, or locales is entirely coincidental.

This book was printed in the United States of America.

To order additional copies of this book, contact:
Xlibris Corporation
1-888-7-XLIBRIS
www.Xlibris.com
Orders@Xlibris.com

*In the end,
it is not what the eye sees,
that counts;*

it is what the mind perceives.

ONE

The great white owl nervously adjusted his stance on the tall pine, sensing something he could not see. The ends of his feathers flicked easily about in the early morning air as he swiveled his head in seemingly total arcs searching, searching for an answer to his uneasiness. Perturbed by the continued pulsing of his warning system, yet failing to find the reason for being awakened at the edge of dawn, he decided to leave his perch. Pushing his wings in great thrusts, he quickly reached the safety of height above the dry, boulder-strewn old riverbed below. With his wings outstretched to their limits, the owl scanned the dried grass and weeds for a meal to compensate for being awakened. Seeing nothing, he flew on toward the dam that dominated the surrounding landscape, where, uncaring and uncomprehending, he watched as the three gates at the right side of the mighty structure erupted into vulgar violence.

Immediately great gushes of greenish-blue water sought release and freedom from the massive reservoir behind, spurred on by the continuing repercussions of the detonating explosions. As the full weight of the 286,000 acre feet of water came to life, it rushed forward, faltered briefly at the constriction where the gates had been, then turned its full might loose over the spillway, hurtling and crashing to the riverbed below.

The echoes of the water-muffled explosions briefly reached the owl as they wafted between the hills on either side of the dam. They were quickly absorbed by the ever-increasing din of the huge reservoir of water fighting, fighting to be on its way to the ocean, thirty miles to the west.

The huge, black steel gates had been blown clear of their supporting columns, their clean, graceful lines, marred and bent forever by the string of explosions at their backs. One lay on top of an oak tree, its full weight bending and crushing the big tree almost flat. The middle gate had bounced and skidded down the spillway, coming to a brief rest on the riverbed below before being scooped up by the on-rushing water and thrown to the top of the lead wave. The remaining gate had been twisted and thrown to the left onto the granite face of the earth-filled dam, sliding slowly down the boulders to the bottom of the incline, where it finally stopped, scarred and humbled.

Two miles downstream, Harold Bursten was awakened by the strange noise and the sudden barking of his dogs. Raising his head off the pillow, he listened intently through the open window above the headboard, trying to determine what he was hearing. His wife, Charlotte, stirred beside him.

Slowly sitting up, she too, cocked her head toward the open window. As she moved to get closer to her husband, the loud pitch of the noise outside stopped her in mid-motion, suddenly causing her to get up and grab her robe from the chairback a few steps away. Putting it on as she half ran for the bedroom door, she called over her shoulder for him to join her in finding out what it was. He quickly complied, putting on his own robe and slippers before running to catch up with her as she headed for the front door.

The Bursten's small ranch straddled the Rio Tranquilo riverbed. Long since dry because of the dam, the riverbed was now only a 40-foot wide depression adding character to their property.

As Bursten caught up to his wife outside the house, the noise they heard to the east was now almost deafening. Their dogs ran to join them, but their barking could not be heard over the onrushing din.

She screamed her question in his ear, but he could only shake his head in wonder. Then, grasping her by the elbow, he started moving again. The roar of the noise increased, punctuated by the sounds of uprooted trees being torn apart. He suddenly stopped. Wide-eyed with terror, he stared at his wife, then grabbed her close to both hug and yell the answer in her ear.

Stunned by his terrifying conclusion, she wrapped her arms around him and screamed an obscenity at those who had constructed the dam. Then, breaking the embrace, she pulled and tugged his rigid body into running back with her towards the house.

Straying from the riverbed, the water pounded and crashed towards the two, clearly visible in the dawn's early light. With its hammerhead crested by the once mighty gate and plumed with a garland of tree branches, it reached out for the stricken, running figures. Terror gripped their legs and bodies, each step an eternity of distance. Their feet became leaden, as if held to the ground, yet they were running faster and faster, spurred on by panic. She still led, he racing to stay close, if not take the lead. In her haste she slipped, almost taking them both down, but he held his balance and jerked her back into an upright position. On they ran, hand-in-hand, seeking safety. All to no avail – the house and refuge were beyond their reach.

The dogs, running nearby, were the first to be caught. Her eyes followed them for a moment as she braced herself against the violent, swirling pressure surrounding her legs. Then, hopelessly, she stopped and turned to face the overwhelming and relentless onslaught.

Suddenly there was silence; eerie silence, as the water enveloped them and immediately slammed them towards the outside wall of their living room. Collapsing under the deluge, the entire house disintegrated as the hungry mass gorged itself on everything in its path.

Continuing to race unobstructed through the ranch, it swooped down on a group of running sheep, devouring them in seconds. Then, as it amassed more power from the emptying reservoir, the destructive force increased its strength and speed, seemingly flexing its muscles for an attack on the two-lane bridge a few miles ahead.

* * *

Clarene Davis found herself racing to reach the lead wave of the onslaught, as if it were a runaway team of frothing horses. Watching their heads emerge and then disappear again into the foam, she repeatedly grabbed for their reins, only to have the leather lines slip through her fingers, seemingly non-existent.

Then, as she braced herself against being carried away by the violent rush, she was suddenly thrust awake in a profusion of perspiration between crumpled and twisted sheets, far from harm's way.

Heart pounding, she took a few moments to orient herself and settle down. In her professional career as a Psychic, she had had many premonitions, but this one had left her whole body tensely quivering. Shaking her head in disbelief at the cascading violence she had seen, she forced herself to recall the terror while the vivid dream remained fresh in her mind.

As she did, she committed as many of the details to her conscious memory as she could, for she knew what it meant when she had seen herself trying to grab the reins – she knew that she must prevent this disaster from happening!

TWO

Friday Morning

Clarene drummed the fingers of her right hand on the nightstand as she held the phone to her ear, waiting impatiently for Victor Alexander to answer. She found the intermittent ringing irritating and wondered where he could be. She hadn't been able to go back to sleep and when the morning light finally began to fill her bedroom, had gotten up for the day. Now, showered and dressed, she anxiously called Victor at home. It was 7:00 a.m.

The ringing stopped abruptly. "Yes?" Victor demanded into the phone. "Who is it?" No hint of having been just awakened in that tone. No, he'd been up already and had ignored the ringing as long as he could.

"It's Clarene!" she said, tersely. "I need to talk! I had a premonition last night, a chilling dream."

"Go on." The voice was now calm, receptive.

"There were explosions. The gates of a dam were blown up. Tons of water escaped, demolishing everything in its path – trees, cattle, dogs, a ranchhouse, people; it was terrible!" Her voice started to climb to the higher pitch it always reached when she got excited.

"Where's the dam? When's it going to happen?" He asked pointedly.

"I don't know! That's the problem. I haven't got a clue."

"How about time? Any indication as to how long before it happens? In days? Or weeks?"

"It could be hours for all I know!" she snapped, full of exasperation. "You know how it is in this business – timing is something we can't nail down. I'd be rich if I could! Anyway, no matter how much time is left, it's already started to run out. We've got to get moving!"

"We? What do you want *me* to do? You're the one that solves crimes for the Sheriff. I'm no good at that sort of thing." He was instinctively reluctant to be drawn into the matter any further.

"Victor!" Her voice was emphatic. "Why do you do that to me? After all the years we've been together, I think I'm entitled to ask for your help when I need it! This is very serious."

Victor's measured breathing punctuated his silence as he stifled a sarcastic response.

Clarene was in no mood to wait for an answer, barely stifling her anger as she issued her order, "I'm heading for the Institute. Meet me there as soon as you can." She started to slam the receiver down for emphasis, but, instead, controlled her voice and firmly added, "People are in danger, Victor. You know I have to try to stop it and you know you have to help!"

* * *

An hour later, as she waited in the parking lot of the Institute for New Age Studies, Clarene's impatience had simmered down. She was still uneasy, though, as she waited in her old, black El Dorado for Victor to arrive. Drumming her fingers on the steering wheel, she hoped it wouldn't be much longer.

A few minutes later, with renewed impatience, she began to

question the need to involve him at all. *Why did I call him?* she angrily chastised herself. *Why am I using him as a crutch? I don't really need him. Besides, he can be such an arrogant ass at times.*

She stared through the windshield, looking at the beige, stucco exterior of the large, one story building that housed the Institute. Unconsciously, her eyes drifted up past the windows to its Spanish tiled roof and then down and over the neatly trimmed low hedge that surrounded its L-shaped exterior.

I keep him on, though, don't I? she answered herself, head nodding in concurrence. *And, why not? There are damn few men out there who understand and can teach new age concepts and Victor is one of them. He's also an expert in past life regressions and that brings lots of new students to the Institute. Besides, whom else can I talk to? I don't have many friends – everyone thinks I can see right into them – and those few that are close enough for me to confide in, would only be disturbed by the premonition. No, Victor is the only one, since he is a Psychic in his own right, even if he doesn't do readings.*

The squeal of tires hastily turning into the driveway near the far corner of the building grabbed her attention. Jerking her head around, she watched the aging gray Volvo dart across the asphalt parking lot and nose to a halt in the space next to hers.

Victor looked over and raised his hand in a simple greeting, then opened the door and eased his short, stocky frame out of the driver's seat.

Clarene got out too, smiling as she waited for him to join her. "Hi, there," she said, bending slightly to give him the obligatory hug of spiritual love. With heels on, she could clearly see the growing bald spot through the finely textured black hair at the center of his head. "Thanks for coming."

"It sounds ominous," he responded without a hint of complaint about having been forced to be there.

"You're right about that," she said, as they walked to the

side entrance. "It left me in a frazzle. The bed was all torn up and I was covered with perspiration."

The side entrance towards which they headed was covered with a short, arched, brown canvas awning that was more decorative than functional. Clarene unlocked and held the door open for Victor as they entered the pleasant pink and white room that served as the Institute's social area.

She knew what she had to do to get his cooperation, yet was apprehensive of being able to pull it off without fireworks being generated between them. She'd dealt with him for too long, not to know that.

"Let me tell you what I want, Victor," she said, as the door automatically closed behind them. "There's no doubt I have to prevent it from happening. But, no matter how much I tried this morning, I couldn't get past the details of the disaster itself. I couldn't begin to pinpoint the when's and where's. That's why I called you. I want you to use your abilities – go over the details with me and see if you can gain some sense of time and place about this premonition."

She knew full well that to panic and thrash away at the situation without facts or substance would be useless, time consuming and aggravating. No, indeed, she needed a firm hand and solid guidance to see her through the beginning of this process!

"Sure," he replied in a voice full of cooperation. "Do you want to do it here or in your office?" He gave her a smile that said she was forgiven for involving him and at the same time asked to be forgiven for his reticence.

"Let's stay here," she said. "I feel like having some tea. Want some?" She felt better, now. She had counted on his sense of loyalty prevailing, for she knew the eccentric mannerisms of their working relationship provided the very glue that held it together.

She pointed for him to sit at one of the round tables, then went into the adjoining kitchen to microwave two cups of water.

He watched her on the other side of the wide, pass-through counter that separated the two rooms, admiring the elegance of her light red tailored suit and the way it complemented her orangish-red hair. He marveled at how young and graceful she still looked at fifty-six. To him, her tall, well-proportioned body and the softly shaped, caring features of her face showed little signs of age. *Capricorn's are that way,* he thought. *Always older when they're young, and forever young when they grow older. Too bad we Cancers can't claim the same advantage.*

He continued to watch her, even as he removed his bifocals and began to clean them with his tie. When he was finished, he put them back, carefully adjusting them on the pudgy nose protruding from his round, stocky face.

Clarene returned and placed the steaming cups on the table, then handed him a teabag as she sat down to open her own.

"Nice jacket," she said, pointing to the tan, summer weight sport coat he was wearing. "New?"

"Finally broke down and got it last week. With summer here, I knew I'd need it, even though I can't really afford it."

She ignored his comment. "Looks nice. I'm sure you'll be getting all gussied up with new slacks and shoes, next." She couldn't stand the sight of the rumpled slacks he always wore, and she knew without looking that his shoes needed shining.

Watching her eyes and sensing her critical evaluation, Victor cut off any further comments with a sudden question. "What kind of a setting is the dam in?"

"Wide open country," she quickly answered. "I can visualize it all. Foothills on either side, leading up to a low mountain range. Dry riverbed below the dam. Lots of dark blue water behind it."

"Describe what you see, tell me about the dam," he said, dunking the tea bag in his cup.

"It's straight, massive and made of dirt faced with huge granite rocks. There's a road on top that leads to three immense gates on the right side."

"Are you looking at it from the front?"

"Yes. The lake is behind it."

"What time of year is it?"

"I'd say it was summer. The grass and vegetation are generally brown and dry, except for right around the lake."

"Feels like California. Is it?"

"There are a lot of oak trees around. The foothills are like what you'd see in a typical California coastal range, covered with chaparral and the usual outcroppings of rocks. I can make out a scattering of taller trees, probably pines, on the higher slopes. Yes. I'd agree it was California."

"What's the source of the water for the lake?"

"I can't visualize that far beyond the dam, but I suspect there's a river of some sort coming from the hills."

"What time of day is it?"

"Early. The edge of morning. The first rays of the sun are already backlighting the mountains. I can make out most everything, except in the dark shadows."

"Why is someone going to blow the dam up?" It was an abrupt question designed to trigger the first response that came to her mind — a technique he often used to unblock and reach a valid answer.

It caught her off-guard, as he hoped it would, but she could only shake her head. "I don't know…I just don't know. *I do know* that when the enormous power of all that water gets going, it's is going to destroy a lot of things, probably even more than what I saw in my dream." Her voice started to rise; "It's just too much for me to sort out right now, Victor. That's why you're here."

She looked at him intently. "I know you've been seeing images in your mind as I spoke – you have wonderful talents. What have you picked up so far?"

"I see a dark-haired young woman and a gray-haired old man."

Clarene folded her arms and waited, her eyebrows raised in anticipation of hearing the details. A moment or two passed.

Victor fidgeted, then shrugged his shoulders to stop her from starring. "That's it. That's what I got."

"A dark-haired young woman? A gray-haired old man?" she said, sarcastically. "That's it? No depth, no feelings as to why she or he is involved? Good god, Victor, what kind of a psychic are you?"

He shook his head defensively, "Hey, do you want me to make up stories? I'm sorry, I can't. That's the only images I can get from you at the moment – nothing else is getting through! You're concentrating so hard about trying to stop it, that you're blocking everything else! Why don't you go to your office and meditate? Go and relax, cool down, then we can get back to it."

She nodded her head in agreement. "Maybe I should," she said, standing up. "I *really am* getting edgy and fretful about this, aren't I?" A wave of guilt passed over her as she looked at him. "I'm sorry for the way I've acted. It's just that I feel the dream was given to me so I could prevent it and now I'm frustrated that the details aren't there to guide me."

She shook her head slowly, dejectedly, then abruptly asked the question she desperately wanted *him* to answer: "Do you have *any* feel for when this will all come together? Do I *have* time to stop it?"

He shook his head, perplexed, knowing she too, was trying to jar the answer out of him. "No. I'm sorry, but I don't."

"Come on, Victor!" she pleaded. "I need your help!" She brought her face down to his. "People's lives are at stake. Concentrate on it!"

"Damnit, Clarene! I only see images of the young woman and the old man. That's all." He clenched and unclenched his fists. "I'm sure there's more, but that's all I can see now." He stared up at her as he reached for his tea. "Relax. Go meditate!"

Discouraged, she started to walk away from the table, but stopped abruptly as he suddenly called out after her, "You'll know more, very soon."

She whirled to face him. "Why do you say that?"

"I feel the presence of the young woman getting stronger. She will have the key to how much time you have."

"Getting stronger? Is she coming here? Is it one of our students? Is that why the dream was so vivid? How will she know how much time we have?" The questions ran on together until Clarene ran out of breath.

"I don't think we know her," he answered. "I don't see any images of her face in my mind yet, but it doesn't feel like we've met her before. Remember, your dream is tied to the future, and what I'm sensing is tied to your dream. All I can tell you, for sure, is that I feel she will be important to you."

"OK. OK. I know what you're saying," she replied, nodding her head in acknowledgment. She took a step then added dejectedly, "This is not the way it goes when I work with the sheriff. In those cases, the crime's already been committed and they can usually tell me when, where and how. I only have to come up with images of who and why. This thing with the dam is topsy-turvy, the other way around."

She looked at her empty cup on the table. "Time is the issue, Victor! Everyone always wants to know when the things I predict will happen. I don't know any legitimate psychic that can give a precise date or time regarding any prediction, but here I am, demanding to know timing from you. God help me, I'm becoming like one of my own clients." As she started to leave again, she changed her tone, "Let me work on clearing my mind. I'll be back in a while."

"I'll be around," he replied, picking up the cups to take to the kitchen. "By the way, do you have some readings scheduled, or are you all dressed up to do another television show?"

"I've got two readings scheduled this morning. The first one's at ten, with a businessman. I hope I'm up to it." She proceeded into the hallway, ignoring his comment about being dressed up. After all, he knew she always tried to look her best. He, on the other hand, she knew, could use some help in selecting a wardrobe. He wore the same slacks day in and day out, with a tweed sport coat in the fall and winter months and with a lightweight jacket in the spring and summer. At least the one he had on today was new.

She started down the skylighted hallway towards her office in the front of the building, but abruptly turned left through the double doors into the building's former sanctuary, now used as an auditorium. The room gave the impression of being much larger than it was because of its many windows and white walls, all offset by the dark, fake beams in the open ceilings. She always found the spiritual energy concentrated in that room to be invigorating.

It had been three years since the previous owners, a Methodist group, had outgrown the building and decided to sell. She had liked its corner location in the quiet residential neighborhood and had offered her life savings as down payment. Once it had become hers, she had changed the name on the door, converted the sanctuary into a general auditorium and set about creating a center for new age studies.

A few of the neighbors had initially complained to the Mayor and the local newspaper about "that Psychic" and her "New Age Cult" moving in, but had quieted down when articles started appearing about law enforcement agencies using her skills to solve homicides and other major crimes.

The publicity had also brought new clients for her weekday psychic readings, as well as students for the evening classes she offered. She had hoped for greater success, but found herself frequently strapped for funds. She knew few psychics were ever financially independent, but, even at her age, she wanted to be one of them.

When she finally reached her office, she closed the door, slipped off her shoes and settled onto the long, upholstered white couch and closed her eyes. Within moments she was deep in meditation.

* * *

Victor spent a few more moments at the table putting his thoughts together. He then got up and walked through the auditorium on his way to the library – a small cozy room located on the other side of the wall from where he had been in the social area. After opening the curtains on the two corner windows, he unlocked a cabinet at the bottom of one of the tall bookcases and removed the storage box he had placed there the day before. Carrying it to the large, circular reference table, he seated himself and opened it to retrieve his manuscript on *Past Lives Regression*. Since he was here, he may as well work on it, he thought, even though he knew that Clarene would soon return to interrupt him. But, he best take the time he could, since the afternoon would be shot, too, having to prepare for his evening class.

Thumbing through the manuscript, he found the section he wanted. Pencil in hand, he mentally cursed the loss of his computer to a crashed hard drive and the lack of funds to repair or replace it. Handwriting a manuscript was a tedious process. In the long run he knew he would have to pay to get his agent to have it typed. Nevertheless, he quickly became absorbed in his writing.

When he looked up again, he was startled to see Clarene standing next to him, her piercing brown eyes staring intently at his work.

Startled with her presence, he muttered a quick, "You back already? Anything wrong?"

"No. It's been over an hour, Victor, it's almost nine thirty," she said, pointing to her watch. Then, looking at the pile of loose pages, she asked, "How's it coming? Almost ready to publish?"

"It'll be months before I get it done. I originally wrote a 'how-to' manual. Now, the editor says he wants it expanded to include examples of what others have done, and the things they've experienced."

"Good heavens, why?"

"He wants to reach a larger audience. Says there are a lot of people on the fringes of belief about past lives and would need the extra comfort of knowing others have done it and what to expect. At this rate, it'll be a long time before I see any money from it."

"Still paying off Sheila's debts?"

"How I failed to see what she was doing with those credit cards is beyond me," he said, dejectedly. "Love is truly blind, isn't it? But, twenty thousand dollars worth of blind? I was really stupid. That's what I get for marrying a younger woman. Strange karma. I felt so good about it at the beginning – like I'd found my soulmate. But then, material things became so important to her that she forgot about me – except as the guy to pay for them, even though I never had much to start with." Victor shook his head. "Now that we're divorced, I only hope I can forgive her and get on with the rest of my life."

"You will. But it will be easier when the bills are paid."

"I don't think I'll ever trust another woman."

"Don't be bitter, Victor. You've got to learn to trust yourself, first. You've got to learn to give of yourself, too, if you want to get love and attention in return." Her words were meant to be tender, considerate.

Instead, Victor's head jerked up and he looked at her reproachfully. "When I want a reading, Clarene, I'll ask for it." Obviously the words hadn't been taken the way she had intended.

She couldn't help but laugh. It came out high pitched, full of mirth with a tinge of embarrassment at what she had started. "That's no reading, Victor. You wear the words as if they were printed on a sweatshirt." The lines were suddenly drawn between the two without purpose or forethought.

"What is this?" he retorted angrily. "I thought you ordered me here to talk about *your* problems, not mine. Now, all of a sudden you're picking on me." Recharging his lungs, he spewed out his caustic scolding. "Who the hell are you, anyway, to tell me your perception of my faults? You — with your monumental ego, who just had to buy this place as a tribute to your power as a psychic? You — with no man in your life, because they're all terrified to be around you and the way you emasculate them with your psychic superiority? No, Clarene, I don't think you're in a position to offer criticism, and I sure as hell don't need it." He stared at her for a moment, then looked back down to his manuscript. He picked up the pencil and started doodling.

Stunned at the outburst, Clarene started to back away, then stopped. "I apologize, Victor. You should know by now that when I offer insights like that — I do it as a teacher, trying to help you grow in this lifetime. We've done that for each other over many lifetimes."

"That's true," he said quietly, nodding in agreement without looking up. "But this lifetime seems to be more annoying. Maybe it's because you're in the superior role, while I play the underling." He turned his head slightly towards her. "You know I'm generally in tune with your concerns, but don't let this dream — and the mandate you think it gives you to stop the disaster — get out of hand. I can understand your frustration and anger with the circumstances, but we're all each other has. Don't get so wrapped up in it that you forget that."

He smiled at her. It was over as quickly as it had started.

That said, he began to summarize what they knew so far. "We've got an inkling about two of the participants, one a dark-haired young woman and the other a gray-haired old man. I feel the young woman will show up soon, but don't know when. That's not a lot to go on, but I don't think we can do anything else but wait. Searching for her at this point will be nothing more than an exercise in psychic futility, even for someone with your abilities."

"What about the explosives?" she asked, looking for other avenues to pursue. "Can a person easily come by explosives powerful enough to destroy the gates of a dam?"

"They don't have to be that powerful, I think. Ordinary dynamite – which is relatively easy to get – packaged in a watertight container, could probably be exploded underwater. If so, the very weight and mass of the water would hold and direct the explosive force right at the columns, tearing the gates away."

"No help there, then. Any other avenues come to mind?"

"No, none that I can think of," he said, shaking his head. "But, it occurs to me – if you were given the dream so you could do something about it, then you'll be given the tools you'll need, as well. I'm sure that will include learning the time and the place. You're just going to have to be patient and wait for things to develop."

"That's easy for you to say, Victor," she replied slowly. "But, it doesn't feel to me like we have a lot of time. To me, this is *day one* and counting."

THREE

Friday Afternoon

Late that afternoon, not more than a few miles away, Janice Weston closed and locked her desk drawer at the office where she worked. As she reached for her purse, she saw her friend Teri, approaching. "Hi there," she called out to her. "You heading home?"

"Yes, but, I wanted to talk to you first," Teri replied. There was a firmness to her voice.

"Again?" Janice was getting weary of Teri. The subject was always the same.

"I know you're tired of hearing it, but I wanted to remind you – it's the middle of July and the company beach party is a week away. Please, please, take some time this weekend and find a guy to bring as a date."

Janice suppressed a laugh. "Teri, you're a good friend, but you can be such a pain at times! Why can't I just go by myself? Why is it so darned important to bring a date?"

"Because," Teri answered sternly, "You're very attractive and when you go to these things alone, it doesn't look right. Everyone thinks you hate men."

"I don't hate men. They just give me the jitters; they make me feel like I'm being smothered. They always have."

"Look, Janice, we've been friends a long time and I tell you, it's time you faced up to it. An attractive, single woman your age usually has a lot of men in her life. You don't. You're going to be twenty-nine next month. That's why I've been pushing you so hard. Start to do something about it now, so you don't end up single in your old age, when you turn thirty."

"What's wrong with being single?"

"Nothing, if that's what you really want. Is it?"

"What if it isn't? What would you suggest I do? I've asked you that before and all you or the other girls ever say is 'get out and get around; the right guy will show up'. Well, I don't feel like bar hopping and forget about dancing with guys – most of them don't know how. And, I'm not going to just grab the first guy I meet and say 'hey, do you want to go to a beach party with me?'" Janice turned suddenly somber. "So what do you suggest, Teri? What does my office mother want me to do?"

The pleading tone of the question was sincere. Teri took prompt advantage and decided it was the right time to make the suggestion she had been holding back. "As long as you've asked, I'd say forget about the party and concentrate instead on finding out why being around guys makes you so uncomfortable."

"Hey! It's not *that* important to me," Janice replied. "I'm not going to spend money going to a shrink, if that's what you have in mind."

"I was thinking of something a lot more fun."

"Like what?"

"I read an article in the paper a couple of weeks ago about this Psychic that solves homicides for the police. They say she's really good. The paper said she runs an Institute for New Age Studies over in Bellflower. You ought to try it."

"Try what? Solving murders for the police?"

"No! Of course not! I meant, try the class she offers in Past Lives. That's what."

"Past lives?" Janice looked at Teri quizzically, wondering if she was being put on. But, the serious look on her friend's face told her otherwise.

"I'm not sure I *had* a past life, Teri. Besides, what's that got to do with my feelings about men?"

"Oh, come on, Janice. Of course you had a past life. Everyone's had a past life. The big thing is to find out how or why the past life is affecting the way you live this one. It's called karma. You know, what goes around comes around; only it's from one lifetime to another."

"You believe in this?" Janice asked, eyeing Teri with a sense of caution.

"I've been reading up on it. I'm thinking about going, myself."

"Good. Let me know how it turns out." Janice grabbed the opportunity to finish the conversation. She started to leave, but Teri put out her hand. "That class is for *you*. I really think you ought to look into it."

"Because you think something that happened in a past life makes me feel as I do about men in this life?" Janice didn't like or understand that idea at all.

"Yes. And, it will be a lot fun for you to find out!"

Janice knew that once Teri started, she wouldn't stop bugging her, even if it meant involving everyone at the office. She certainly didn't need that aggravation; it was a lot easier to nod her head and concede. She jotted down the address Teri gave her.

"I'll try to go by the place this weekend," she said, putting the address in her purse. "If it feels right, I'll ask about the class." She stood up and slung the purse over her shoulder. "I'll let you know, Monday."

* * *

Saturday

Janice spent most of the day enjoying herself walking the malls and shopping for odds and ends. By late afternoon she was tired. Her feet hurt, her jeans felt too tight and now she had gotten herself lost driving around Bellflower searching for the Institute.

Checking her map book once more, she tried yet another side street and was rewarded when the building appeared as she approached the corner. It's beige exterior and dark brown trim harmonized easily with the profusion of Eucalyptus and flower-laden Jacaranda that dominated the entire block. A width of grass, growing slowly in the shade, extended between the sidewalk and the hedge that abutted the building.

She saw a glass-encased announcement board in the lawn near the corner and drove forward to read it:

PSYCHIC FAIR TODAY
4 TO 8 P.M.
FREE ADMISSION
READINGS $10.00
DINNER $5.00

Afterwards she would not recall that the decision had been so immediate, so effortless. She drove around the corner past the end of the building and turned into the parking lot, catching an empty space.

She sat for a moment getting her bearings, then looked in the rear-view mirror and gave a quick once-over to her hair, cut shorter a week ago than she wanted it to be. *It'll grow back;* she silently hoped and then self-consciously touched the end of her nose. *Expressive,* her friends had called it, but she knew differently, *it's only my grandmother's nose, softened to fit my face!*

Still in all, at 5'6", with deep blue eyes and gently arching eyelashes that accentuated her upper face, she was considered very attractive by both men and women. The soft glow of her skin complemented the highlights in her blond hair, adding to her slim, trim appeal. Many ignored the implications of her petite, but firmly set chin, but not for long.

She straightened the scarf at her throat, got out of the car and walked across the lot toward the open side entrance of the building.

As she got closer, she could see people sitting around tables, talking, while others were standing at a pass-through counter by the kitchen, getting coffee from an urn or selecting food and utensils.

A sudden fear of the unknown grabbed her and she wondered if she were going in the wrong door. An inner force kept her moving, though, although more slowly, up to and finally through the entrance.

A tall woman, wearing a white pants suit, her head topped by a large, circular white summer hat, walked over to her as she entered. "Hello," she said, holding out her hand in greeting, "I'm Clarene Davis."

"Hi," Janice answered, looking first at Clarene and then around the room, as she shook hands. "I'm not sure where to go or what to do. I came by to inquire about classes and saw the sign out front. What's a Psychic Fair?"

"We bring a lot of Psychics together so they can do readings for people. This way you can pick and choose the one you want. Have you ever had a reading?"

Janice shook her head. "No."

"Try it. I think you'll enjoy it. Go over to the booth near the far wall of the auditorium," she said, pointing to the next room. "You can get tickets there for food and a reading. After you sign up for the Psychic you want, come back here and have some dinner." She turned to leave, but stopped. "I'm glad you came. Relax with it and enjoy yourself."

Janice watched her walk into the auditorium. A moment later, an older woman came up to her and placed a hand on her arm. "If you want a reading from her, you'd better hurry. Her sign-up list gets filled first."

"Why? Who is she?" Janice asked.

"She's the Director of the Institute. She's the best. She's also a wonderful person." Pointing toward the ticket tables at the far side of the auditorium, she nudged Janice. "You'd better go now."

Moving through the brightly covered tables where the Psychics were working, Janice kept her eyes on the pastel-colored ticket booth near the outside wall of the auditorium and reached it with ease. Inside the simple wood and paper framework stood a young man.

"Hi," he said, as she approached. "Do you want just a reading or the combo?"

"I don't know. This is my first time here."

Readings are ten dollars and dinner is five. The combo is a dollar less." He beckoned her to the side of the booth. "There are about twenty readers here today," he said. "After you buy your ticket, you sign-up for the one you want and when it's your turn, you go to their table. Some of the readers are more popular, so their lists get filled faster. A reading takes about fifteen minutes. If the reader you want is open right away, take the appointment and eat later. Otherwise eat now and come back at your appointment time. The food's great, and the combo's the best deal."

She pulled a ten and a five from the pocket of her western shirt and handed them over. As he gave her the tickets and the dollar change, he nodded toward the sign-up lists displayed on easel boards next to his booth. "Each of the Psychics has a sign-up board showing their pictures and specialties. Check them over and choose one. Then select an open time slot and write in your name."

"Is Clarene available?"

"Her list filled up as soon as the doors opened at four."

Janice struggled with the lists on the easel boards, reading the enticements for a few:

Naomi – Psychometry and Tarot
William – Numerology
Allison – Clairvoyance, Tarot, Psychometry
Victor – Past Lives
Irma – Palmistry

There were many boards to read, and the words on some were unfamiliar. "I know what Tarot is," she thought outloud, "but what's Psy…com…e…tree?"

"That's where the reader grasps an object," said Clarene, who now stood beside her, "and interprets its energy vibrations into a reading about you. The object could be one of your rings, or a bracelet, or some other personal possession. The readings are generally quite accurate, since the object usually has absorbed a lot of your energy. The longer you've worn it, the more of your energy it's absorbed. I use psychometry a lot in my police work, but I prefer clairvoyance."

Janice looked up at the friendly face, still framed by the white hat, and wondered if Clarene was taking a break between readings.

"Put your name in my six o'clock slot," Clarene gently ordered. "Perry has it now, but he'll understand. I can do a reading for him anytime. That'll give you some time to eat and relax. First times are always a little different, somehow." Turning to leave, she looked back at Janice. "When you were born, your Grandmother called you 'Ja-neece'. You really should pronounce it that way. It fits your individualism."

Janice stood in stunned awe as she watched Clarene move away through the auditorium. At the far end she saw her climb a couple of stairs onto a wide raised dais and then sit down on a large, oriental-style wicker chair, ready for her next reading.

Janice drew a line through Perry's name and overwrote her own, then walked to the social area to get her dinner. The line was short, the food was excellent, but by the time she finished, she found herself becoming fidgety and a bit anxious. *I came here to see about classes,* she thought, *and now look at me, I'm signed up for a reading by a Psychic. I guess there's a first time for everything. How did she know Grandma called me Ja-neece? Nobody outside the family knew that was her pet name for me.*

She kept looking at her watch and when it reached six, got up, dumped her plate and utensils in the trash and walked into the auditorium. The chair opposite Clarene was just being vacated. Hesitantly, Janice walked across the room.

"How's the food tonight?" Clarene asked, as Janice sat down.

"Fantastic. Who's does your cooking?"

"A couple of volunteers. They're always here when you need them, especially for these once-a-month fairs."

Janice leaned forward and intimately asked, "How do you do a reading?" She wasn't concerned, just curious.

"I read for people using clairvoyance – seeing in my mind's eye, past, present or future events involving the person. I also use clairsentience, which allows me to sense or feel information, as well as clairaudience, where I hear words spoken in my mind. Sometimes I read auras too, the energy fields that surround people, by interpreting the colors and patterns."

"How exciting it must be to have all those talents. How long have you been doing it?" Janice asked.

"For many years. I started in my home before I got this place. Everyone tells me I'm very accurate and many of them keep coming back for current readings. A lot of my clients even come for psychic counseling and guidance. But, let's talk about you. I don't usually start with the aura, but yours is very blotched and broken. The colors tend to be made up of shades and variations. I would say your energies are scattered, that you are searching for something in life to hang on to – a goal, a purpose. You desperately want balance, but on *your* terms. You think you are an independent person, but in reality you rely too much on others for direction in your life. The most cohesive color is red, indicating a strong sexual desire, but I feel there's an even stronger sense of foreboding about men that keeps you at a distance from them."

Janice cringed and nervously adjusted her position on the chair. She wasn't sure she liked the idea of someone she'd just met getting this close to the truth right away! She steeled herself as Clarene continued.

"Your job is satisfying and you have a lot of girl friends, but the work is frequently boring. What sort of office management do you do?"

"I'm an administrative assistant in a computing firm. We do out-source work for large companies when they get overloaded."

"You won't be in that job long. I feel there's a change coming for you. Some sort of new job at another company, probably by the end of summer or early in the fall."

"Doing what?"

"It feels like a position of real responsibility, where you get to make decisions on your own. You'll be happy with it because you'll get to use some skills you've acquired, but didn't use before. Did you recently get a degree?"

"Yes. About a year ago. I finally finished my work for a Bachelors in Management. Went nights for a long time."

"Well, that's going to pay off with a better job and more pay." Clarene stopped for a moment, then continued. "Are your parents still on this side?"

"Side of what?"

"Still alive. Are they still with us? It feels like they have either gone over, or you keep them at a great distance."

"I don't have much to do with them. They both think I should be married and raising their grandchildren. They grew up in the seventies with a whole different set of rules. They don't understand me and won't give up trying to change me. We argued a lot. After they moved to Palm Springs, my life calmed down and I didn't see much reason to see them."

"You still want their love and attention, though, but on your terms. That's a reasonable expectation. Give them time; they love you and miss you. It feels like you'll get together for Christmas. It may be a little rough, at first, but with all the positive things going on for you this year, I think you'll be pleased to see them again. This hang-up you have about men, though, is a real problem. Keeps getting in the way of your happiness."

"What can I do about it?"

"You're going to deal with that soon, too."

"How?"

"It feels like you're going to take on some sort of self-awareness project that keeps growing until a whole lot of things are put into their proper place. You'll be anything but lonely by the time it's over."

"Sounds fascinating. Can you tell me more?"

"It'll involve water and a map." Clarene hesitated, just staring at Janice, then added, almost disconcertingly, "It has something to do with this Institute." A moment passed, then Clarene said with a certain finality, "I'm sure the rest will come to us, later."

That was an odd look, thought Janice. Was *she trying to keep something from me?*

"There is joy and happiness in your future," Clarene continued. "I also feel you and I will be close friends, for there is a karmic tie between us."

"Karmic tie? What is that? A friend of mine mentioned karma just this week and I don't think I really know what it is."

"Karma and karmic ties are related to those situations involving people we've known before, through past lives. Some karma is good, like renewing old friendships and carrying them to new levels. Other karma involves the opportunity to once again learn a lesson that was previously rejected. A lot of lessons are hard to accept and we keep fighting them, but they keep coming back time after time, until we learn them."

"Is that why some people keep having the same kind of problem over and over – the lesson is there to be learned, but the person keeps rejecting it?"

"Absolutely. One of the things we teach here is how to handle karma. We strive for unconditional acceptance of one another, but we're also realistic enough to recognize that each of us has our own path to travel to reach that goal."

Janice instinctively understood what Clarene was saying and unconsciously nodded her head in agreement.

Clarene leaned back in the wicker chair. "These psychic fairs are our way of introducing people to what we are and what we can do for them. Most people aren't ready to develop further, so they come out only for monthly fairs. Others are ready to develop spiritually and come back for the basic and advanced classes."

"I think I'd be interested in your classes," said Janice, responding to the subtle invitation.

"Do you ride a horse?" Clarene asked abruptly.

"No. I've never cared for horses or riding. Why?"

"Just something I picked up. Saw you riding double with a man on a horse, across open, parched land. Odd situation though, like you might be in danger."

"How did you see that?" Janice looked incredulously at Clarene. "I have a nightmare like that. I've had it since I was a little girl. It usually comes when I'm under pressure, you know, stress." Janice started to breathe faster, the images of the nightmare darting through her mind. "I don't like horses, they scare me. The man on that horse really scares me. I always wake up in a cold sweat, fearing the worst."

"Have you had that nightmare lately?"

"The last time was about a year ago. It's always the same, though. I'm sitting behind a dark-haired young man who seems to be Mexican. I've got my arms wrapped around him, yet I know if I stay with him, we'll both be killed."

"How do you know that?"

"It's a deep, scary feeling. I start to feel smothered and I know I have to get off the horse. But before I can, I always wake up in a cold sweat."

She had never told anybody about the dream, not even her parents, for fear they would laugh at her. Now that it was out in the open, she tried to be humorous about it with Clarene. "I always had the feeling it was telling me not to get involved with the wrong man. Trouble is, it scared me so much, I never found the time to find the right one."

"Next time you have that nightmare, try to remember as many details as you can. I can tell you there's a lot more there than just a fear of being with the wrong guy. I think you ought to pursue it further."

"Is that the self-awareness project you mentioned earlier?"

"Yes, it could be. That seems to be a good place to start."

"I'm not sure I want to open that dream up. But, if I decide to, will you be there to help?"

"Of course. I said we were going to become close. Maybe that's the way." Clarene looked past Janice's shoulder. "I see the next person waiting over there and our time's up. Do you have any quick questions about the reading?"

"None and a million more." Janice said, emitting a quick laugh. "Where can I get information about your classes?"

Clarene reached down beside her chair. "Here's our brochure. Call me or just come back. Our hours are listed in there."

Stuffing it in her purse as she got up, Janice looked at her watch and was surprised to see that seventeen minutes had gone by. Looking back at Clarene, she said, "It would be nice to have you as a friend. Thanks for the reading, I really enjoyed it."

"Don't be lonely this summer, Ja-neece. We've got a lot to keep you busy down here."

Janice smiled as she turned and walked through the auditorium.

* * *

Clarene located Victor in the library. The fair was over; the readers had gone home.

"A young woman came in this evening," she said, walking up to where he was seated at the reference table. "When I first saw her, I had a feeling I should do a reading for her, so I rearranged my schedule. When I did the reading, it came to me that she's the one you predicted yesterday. Only, her hair was blond. The one you saw had dark hair, didn't she?"

"That's the way I saw her in my mind – with dark hair," Victor replied.

"The more I think about it," Clarene went on, "the more I believe what you said yesterday about the dark-haired women being the key to the dream. It feels right to me. You also said her presence was getting stronger and I think the woman I read for is the one – in spite of her having blond instead of dark hair." Clarene cupped her hand around her mouth, visualizing Janice for a moment, then took it away and pointed at Victor. "You know, when I was reading for her, I saw her riding double on a horse across open fields. Her hair was blowing back behind her head and it was dark, not blond."

"Maybe she dyed her hair since then. Ask her, when she comes back."

"I hope she comes back. But, when? This is the end of day two and I still don't know how much time we have!"

"Relax, you're blocking your senses again. She'll be back, probably very soon – probably to take a class. Promise me something, though, when she does. Promise me you won't knock her off her feet, trying to get to the bottom of this whole thing right off the bat!"

"OK, OK. I'll give her as much room as I can," Clarene said, the pitch of her voice rising slightly.

"Good. Do you have her number? Do you want to call her and personally invite her back?"

Clarene grimaced. "I didn't think to get her last name or a

phone number. I was so busy thinking about her being the one you predicted, that it just never occurred to me." She stood there a moment, mentally kicking herself. "It doesn't make any difference, anyway. We both know she'll be back."

"That's what I feel," he said, nodding. "Probably tomorrow."

"We're closed Sundays."

They both laughed.

"You know, Victor," she said, looking at her watch, "Tomorrow's lost. The first time we could see her again would be on Monday." She shook her head in despair as she paced from the table to the bookcase and back several times. "That's day four, Victor, and I don't know how many we have left!"

FOUR

Sunday

The morning light rainbowed through the slowly twisting crystal hanging near the opened window. It touched Janice's eye, then arced away, only to return, again and again, causing her to waken enough to follow the colorful pattern swirling across the walls of her bedroom.

She reached for the covers and tried to pull them back, but they wouldn't budge. Irritated, but not fully awake, she yanked on them again. They still wouldn't move. It took her a moment to realize she had fallen asleep on top of them, fully clothed from the night before.

Slowly waking, she stretched and looked around, letting her bedroom come into full focus. Her brow furrowed in brief puzzlement as she wondered about going to sleep dressed and then remembered Clarene and the Psychic Fair. It all came back. She'd come home after the reading and sat down in the living room for a long time, contemplating the things Clarene had told her. It had been late when she finally went to the bedroom, laying down just to close her eyes for a moment.

Now it was morning. Looking around the room once more, she marveled at the hodgepodge of furniture and knick-knacks she had acquired over the years, then decided to get up and shower.

An hour later, her short blonde hair brushed to a pleasing shape, she finished dressing and made ready for a new day. Grabbing her purse from the top of the dresser, she walked to the kitchen of the small apartment to make some breakfast.

The Institute's brochure, cocked in a corner of the purse, caught her eye. She unfolded it and glanced quickly through the sections on the history and purpose of the Institute, before finding the list of current courses.

One, entitled "Past Lives and How They Affect You" immediately caught her attention. It met for six weeks on Mondays. She read through the course description and then re-read it again. When she started to read it a third time, she realized how excited she was getting. But, this wasn't like her – she didn't just jump into things. Something inside told her to be careful. Slow down!

But she didn't. Instead, her eyes were drawn to the dates and times the class would be held. She caught her breath, then looked at the calendar on the wall to confirm what she had just read – she could start tomorrow evening!

Pleased, she went to the refrigerator and pulled out the bagels and a tub of cream cheese. Grabbing a glass, she poured some orange juice and then plugged in the coffeepot.

* * *

Monday

It was a boring morning for Janice, slow from the start. She dodged Teri's questions, saying only that she had found the place and would probably go back. The subject of enrolling in the Past Lives class was not mentioned nor pursued.

The afternoon dragged, too. At the end of the day, she raced home, ate quickly and was ready to go to the Institute by six o'clock, even though classes didn't start until seven. Pointing her late model Camero south, she left her apartment in Downey for the fifteen-minute drive on city streets to Bellflower.

When she reached the Institute's parking lot, she was embarrassed to find it empty, save for the gray Volvo parked in the second space from the side door. She parked in the third space. Not wanting to be the only other person in the building, she sat outside in the car waiting for others to arrive.

A few minutes later, a tap on her car roof startled her back from daydreaming. It was the older woman she'd met in the social area on Saturday.

"Hi. I'm Helen," the woman said through the open window. "You must be Janice. No need to sit out here. You're always welcome to come in early. One or two of us are usually around and we always have some tea or punch made."

Janice waited for the woman to step back, then opened the door to get out. "Thanks. I wasn't sure what to do. The only other car was that one."

"Oh, that's Victor's. He's one of the teachers. Some of the people park on the street. Some, like myself, don't drive; I only live about a block from here. This is my second home. I help out by keeping things organized for Clarene."

"Are there classes tonight?" Janice was still bothered by the empty parking lot.

"Oh, yes. Everyone shows up about seven. We usually get started on time. It's a relaxed atmosphere and we have a lot of fun."

"How many are in the classes?"

"Oh, usually about ten per class, sometimes as many as fifteen. We'll pick up a few stragglers next week and then close it off 'till the start of the next sessions. Clarene said to be on the lookout for you. Said you'd be back."

"Is she here?"

"Not right now. I think she finished up her last reading around five thirty and went home for a little dinner. She's usually back in time, though."

"Reading? Is that the same kind of reading I got the other night at the fair?"

"Oh, no. The ones she does for her clients last for around an hour. She tapes them and goes into a lot of detail. I think the last one was for a school teacher, but she reads for all kinds."

Walking as they talked, they quickly reached the side entrance and entered the social area where Janice sat down at the nearest table. She wondered what the front entrance was like, since she been coming and going only through the side door. As Helen went into the kitchen, Janice noticed a man walking towards her from the direction of the auditorium. He was fairly tall with close-cropped dark hair, a small mustache and a definite, no nonsense look to his firm, but attractive face.

He came over to Janice's table, just as Helen returned with two cups of cold punch. Smiling at him as she handed one of the cups to Janice, she made the introductions. "Bill, this is Janice...what's your last name, dear, I don't know it."

"Weston. I'm Janice Weston."

"Well, Janice, this is Bill Edwards. He's with the Sheriff's Department."

They shook hands. Janice looked at his face and wondered what a Sheriff was doing at the Institute.

"First time here?" he asked.

"No," she responded. "I came last Saturday for the Fair."

"That's a good way to start. I did that a couple of years ago. I was driving by and got curious. Came in and began asking questions. Clarene and I have been working together ever since."

"Working together?"

"I work in homicide at the Sheriff's Department. Clarene has worked with me on several cases. She has the ability to provide insight that's not always available from the evidence."

"Are you working with her on something tonight?"

"No. I'm here for the Past Lives class."

"You take classes, too?" Janice seemed surprised.

"Sure. My boss was very skeptical about my working with her until she did a private reading for him in his office. No one knows what she said to him, but after that, I got the OK to use her on some really tough cases. The only stipulation was that I learn as much about her business as I could, so I could explain what she was doing, in terms he could understand. So, I started taking classes."

"How many have you taken?" asked Janice, curiously drawn to him.

"Four, before this one. Introduction, Intermediate and Advanced New Age Concepts and one on Self-Hypnosis. As I said, this time I'm in the Past Lives class."

"I'm going to take that one, too..." her words dropped off as she hesitated. "Gosh, with all the classes you've taken, does that mean I shouldn't be in it, without taking the others first?"

"No, no, of course not." He smiled, remembering how naive he too, had been at the start. "It isn't necessary. It might be easier if you had the Introduction class first, so you can understand why people are trying to get in contact with a past life. But, a lot of people go directly into the past life class without taking any others and have a lot of fun. Have you been involved with new age concepts before?"

"I'm not sure I even know what that means."

Bill nodded his head, "Would you like me to give you a quick start?"

"Yes, sure." She looked at her watch. "But, I don't want to miss class."

"You won't. This'll be short. New Age, in a broad sense, is a modern packaging of the metaphysical concepts that have been around since Aristotle's time in ancient Greece. The word metaphysical literally means 'beyond the natural or physical' and the idea is to learn how to get beyond the natural, physical restrictions seemingly placed on us at birth. The philosophy is that *you can* get past the limitations you think exist – by taking charge of your own life, instead of life being in charge of you."

Janice couldn't help from commenting, "A lot of people are pushing that idea in books and on TV programs."

"That's true. But, Clarene formed this Institute with the goal of giving people personal, hands-on insight into how they have made themselves into what they are today – and how they can change themselves for a better tomorrow. A lot of people say they are the victims of circumstances. But, the other side of that coin is that there are no victims, that all of us are living life exactly the way we *have created it for* ourselves."

"That's a little hard to accept."

"Probably so. But, nevertheless, essential to the process of understanding the affect past lives have on us. You might want to consider taking the Intro class, too, since it will help raise your level of consciousness."

"It'll do what?"

"It'll help you get in touch with your real inner self. Find out who you are in this lifetime, so you can better understand those things you come in contact with about a past lifetime."

Janice's deep blue eyes narrowed as she stared at him. "You sure don't sound like any cop I've ever known. You're spouting this stuff like you're a paid promoter. Are you sure you're with the Sheriff's Department?"

Bill laughed and pulled out his wallet "Sorry. I get carried away at times. Here's my badge and ID."

Janice looked at it closely, matching the picture on the ID with the man in front of her. Still skeptical, she said, "Do you talk this way around the station?"

"No. I'm in my work environment, there. Some of it inevitably comes through, though, and I get a hard time for it. I believe it helps me to understand the kinds of situations and people I encounter in my job. The classes will help you, too."

"I'm looking forward to them."

"Good. Are you eager to find a past life?"

"I'm not sure. I've got a friend at work who believes in past lives and pushed me toward this class. I came down on Saturday to find out what the class was about and ended up getting a reading from Clarene. The next thing I knew, I decided to sign up for the class. I guess I'm bored with life and looking for a major change in my lifestyle. I'll see how much interest I have in finding a past life, tonight."

"Have you ever been hypnotized?" he went on, full of questions.

"Yes. In college. I was scared the first time, but it was a lot of fun. The next time it happened, I was more relaxed."

"At a party?"

"No. Both times were in a psychology class. The Instructor was demonstrating how post-hypnotic suggestions worked. As I said, it was fun."

"It sounds like you went under easily."

"Yes. He said I was a good subject."

"You'll probably do all right in the Past Lives class, then. I understand the teacher, Victor, uses a form of subtle self-hypnosis that's very effective. I think you'll enjoy it."

He watched her closely, not wanting the conversation to end. Then, catching himself staring, he quickly recovered. "By the way," he said, "if you have any questions you don't want to ask out loud in class, let me know, I'll be happy to try and answer them for you."

Janice smiled at him. She liked talking to him. He was nice, friendly and helpful even though he was a cop. Then the voice from inside came again, cautioning her to be careful, that her life was suddenly changing too quickly. Why the next thing she might do is ask him to the company picnic! She laughed to herself. Fat chance of that. She was going to that picnic by herself, even if it's just to prove a point to Teri.

Helen stood at the door between the hallway and the social area. Speaking loudly enough for everyone to hear, she said, "I've checked the rooms, they're ready. The Past Lives class will be held in Classroom Four. For those who haven't been here before, go down the hallway past the kitchen and the rest rooms. Turn right at the corner and go to the end. Victor's on his way there, now. You people who signed up for self-hypnosis are in Classroom Three. Clarene will be there shortly."

The social area emptied and Janice followed Bill to Classroom Four, listening to him chatter about Victor as they walked. As they turned right at the end of the hallway she glimpsed, off to the left, the front entrance and a door marked **OFFICE**.

Once in the classroom, she paid her fee and stood with the others, leaning against the lavender colored walls, waiting for Victor to start. The thick, royal blue carpet provided a feeling of luxury to the room. There were no chairs, but stacked in the corners were piles of colorful, floral patterned chaise lounge pads.

"This class is not for the timid," Victor said, as he stood at the front of the room. "You are embarking on an adventure that requires your concentration and commitment. The rewards are proportional to the energy you invest.

"For those of you who have been with me before, this will be old hat. I'm sure you'll want to jump right in. Bear with me, though, while I bring our new classmates up to speed.

"In this class, we will use a form of controlled, deep meditation to achieve contact with past lives. In this process, you will be guided by me to visualize a pleasant set of surroundings. Within those surroundings you will find opportunities to see and follow whichever past life experiences you select.

"The purpose of all this is to help you recognize, accept and clear away karma brought into this lifetime from another. We want you to understand why you feel the way you do about certain events or situations that can't be explained from current life experiences. And, when you do begin to understand the real reasons, you'll be surprised how easy it will be to change your feelings and attitudes, as you begin to clear the karma."

Janice looked at Victor, wondering how long he had been at this. She thought him to be at least sixty, judging from his potbelly and stooped shoulders. From what Bill had told her coming down the hallway, he was an expert in the subject of past lives and a respected teacher in the field. Bill also told her Victor had been in the Navy, but had detested the lack of privacy of shipboard life and transferred out of sea duty to some other branch. He wasn't sure which one.

Victor continued with class preparations. "Everyone take a lounge pad and drop it on the carpet. There's plenty of room, so give yourself some space. Lie on your back and get comfortable."

Janice took a light-blue, floral printed pad and looked for a place to put it.

"Over here." Bill invited her to an open space, near him.

"Get yourselves into comfortable positions on the pads," Victor directed, as he turned the wall dimmer to bring the hanging lights to a soft ambiance. "Loosen any tight fitting clothing and remove your shoes."

Janice laid back on the pad, surprised at how comfortable it was, and listened as soft meditative music began playing in the background. Victor spoke again, "Spend a few moments now, cleansing your mind, your body and your soul of negativity. Balance yourself with the positive energy of this room."

Janice wasn't sure how to do that, but found herself mentally sweeping up with a broom.

"Start to relax...relax...relax. See yourself sitting on the edge of a warm, inviting spa. Dangle your feet into the swirling water and feel the warmth begin to climb through your legs, into your body. Know that the warmth carries strong, positive energy that cleanses and purifies as it expands into all the spaces of your inner body and self. Open your crown chakra and let the negative energy flow out of your body as it is pushed aside."

Janice didn't have any idea what a crown chakra was, but since this was a pleasant experience, she decided to mentally create a hole in the top of her head and let the pent up negativity get out anyway it could. She giggled to herself as she thought about what she was doing and hoped no one else heard her.

Victor continued to intone his relaxation technique, each word carrying warm, positive energy into the class. Janice actually felt the tension being released from her body and mind, all the way from her toes upward. By the time Victor completed the process, she was totally relaxed.

Victor's voice was firm, but softly distant. "We are here to get in touch with ourselves. Not as we are today, but as we were in our lifetimes of the past. In reaching ourselves as we were then, we also reach ourselves as we have become now.

"Look for familiar or normal situations. It is not likely you will have had a role as a great historical figure, so ignore any such semblance. Almost all humans have been born into ordinary circumstances and faced ordinary joys and conflicts – conflicts that are and were resolved with ordinary actions and results. It is within those ordinary actions that you will find your karma and the affect it is now having on your life.

"For those who have not experienced getting into a past life, I can only say, let it flow. Let your inner self take you where it will – it knows best where you should go. If you find yourself with something you don't like, just walk away. It's all right to do that. Just tell yourself you want to be back here in this room on your pad, and you will be." His voice dropped off for a moment before softly starting again.

"We'll start in a quiet forest. Feel yourself being there. There is a small blue lake in the near distance. It is late afternoon and the sun is going down behind the mountains beyond the lake. It is very tranquil – you are at peace with yourself and this place. You are on a path, slowly walking towards the lake. Birds are chirping in the trees and you feel a gentle breeze across your face. The path is smooth, for many others have come before to find the same solitude and enjoyment you now seek."

The scene enveloped Janice. She could smell the pines in the forest and hear the birds singing their songs as she walked along the path.

"You have reached the edge of the lake now. There is no one else around. You and your inner self are drawn closer and closer to the clear, blue water. This is a special lake. Reach down and touch the water. Taste it. It is cool and refreshing. It will restore your memories of the past. It will reflect those memories on its surface for you to see. There is nothing to fear from the lake. You live in the present. All that has gone on in your past is there to help you learn about yourself and the purpose of life in the present. Be objective about what the lake shows you – for no matter how real it may seem to be, it is past and gone. Look at the lake closely now. See your image reflected back to you." Victor became quiet for a few moments, then went on. "Now, let that image begin to change into whatever form it wants to become. Let it go, to become as you were at another time. Flow with it, let yourself become part of what you see and feel and hear."

Janice was drawn deeply into the scene she saw, watching it change, slowly, dreamlike, to become a vivid landscape of hard, cracked adobe, dominated by large clumps of wild grass meagerly grasping existence wherever they could. The sharply defined mountains she had first seen around the lake were now shorter, more rounded. The tall pines of the forest had been replaced by images of scattered, shorter oaks and sycamores mingled with chaparral everywhere on the surrounding hills. The sky was clear, its blueness accentuated with puffs of white clouds. In the distance, wisps of smoke fingered their way upward from a dark gray building near the center of a grove of oak trees.

As she looked around the scene, she saw a dark-haired, handsome, young, bearded Mexican stuffing a leather pouch into his saddlebag. When he finished, he reached down and grabbed the loose end of a long rope and tied it to his saddle horn. Following the rope with her eye, she saw the other end was tied around a small, sturdy, wooden crate. She watched in fascination as he mounted the reddish-brown, hairy-legged mustang. He quickly reined it away as if running from danger, only to turn back towards her a second later. Reaching down, he grabbed her around the waist and pulled her awkwardly over the rope and onto the horse behind him. She felt the pain as the saddle bruised her rump, but had no time to cry out as he suddenly galloped off toward the foothills. The heavy box skipped across the dirt behind them, chafing the rope up and down on the inside of her leg. She desperately held onto his waist, trying to catch her breath as the horse pounded its hooves into the hard clay.

The wind blew past her face, blowing her black hair into a ripple behind her head. She clung tighter to him, exhilarated, yet afraid. She looked back over her shoulder and saw a coach and a team of horses standing in the hot afternoon sun. A group of four or five men stood next to it, wildly pointing at her.

She soon lost sight of them, though, as the young Mexican took the horse over a small rise and down to a dry riverbed. They slowed a bit, but maintained a steady pace, less hurtful to her leg now for the rope had ceased whipping up and down. She maintained her tight grasp around him, though, making no effort to get away.

The foothills were getting closer. The sky was very blue and she concentrated on it in an effort to forget the pain in her leg. It very blueness reminded her of the lake where she had started, a lake which then slowly materialized and replaced the scene she had been watching. In the distant reaches she could hear a voice.

"Come back now. Come back now to the lake…let it slowly change back to the present. The sun is behind the mountains and the breeze across the lake refreshes you. Turn away from the lake now and take the path back to the trees. You are relaxed and at peace with yourself. You have seen part of your past at the lake and if you choose, you may bring the memory back with you into the present." Victor's voice was soothing, gentle, guiding her back.

"Come back now to this time and place. You are at peace. Blink your eyes a few times and then keep them open."

Janice found it hard to keep her eyes open. It had been so pleasant at the lake that she wanted to stay. Still, after a moment or two, she responded and opened her eyes.

"How many of you experienced something when you looked into the lake?" Victor asked. "I know many of my former students did, so I'm more interested in what any of the new students might have seen."

Janice started to raise her hand, but stopped in embarrassed silence, wondering if it was worth telling or not. Bill reached out to encourage her to go on, but she couldn't. Instead, she began to relive the experience in her conscious mind, seeking to bond it there.

Two or three others shared their experiences before Victor spoke again. "Let's go back to the lake now. Get yourselves in a comfortable position and see yourself…"

Janice heard no more. She continued to relive her experience, trying to fix it in her mind. It had been so real to her, the same as her dream, but without the fear. She was exhilarated and wanted to go back, but not now. No, she wanted to talk to Clarene about it, first!

* * *

Clarene and Victor stood together in the center of the classroom. "Were you able to home-in on what she was experiencing?" Clarene asked.

"No. But, I had a very strong indication something was going on, so I brought the class back from the lake. I thought she was going to share it with us, but she got embarrassed and kept quiet."

"Where was her pad?"

"Right over there." Victor pointed to the spot. Clarene stepped over and knelt down. She slid her hand around on the carpet, sensing for latent psychometric energy.

"There's not much here. Just something about a Spanish Mission and Mexican soldiers in the early days of California. It's not clear what the connection is, though. What time frame would that be? The early nineteenth century?"

"I think so. The Mexicans were certainly here then, in fact, all the way through the gold rush."

"Did you pick up anything from her during the class worth pursuing?"

"Not really. There's a lot of students in the class and a lot of energy bouncing off the walls. You're much better at picking out that type of thing than I."

"Right," she said sarcastically, then impatiently added, "Here it is the end of day four and I still haven't got anything of substance to go on."

"Au contraire, Clarene, au contraire. I think you have the roots of it already. She's here and in a few more sessions she's going to hand you the keys. From there on it will all come clear."

"A few more sessions? I don't have time for a few more sessions! If you know that much, then you must see the rest. Tell me now! Quit making me chase my tail!"

He looked at her and laughed.

A moment later her mood changed and she laughed, too. "There I go again, trying to force an answer," she said meekly. "I should learn to wait, to let it to come in its own sweet way."

"Atta girl, don't let your ego get in your way."

"Ah, ego and patience. How nice it would be to have them in balance."

"In your case, it would be boring. You'd lose your endearing personality."

"Do me a favor, will you?" she abruptly asked, changing the subject. "I know you love history – its another of your wonderful Cancerian qualities. See what you can find about the life and times of early nineteenth century California. The date 1820 keeps buzzing through my mind so why not start there? Don't do a lot, just get me a quick summary that will put things in perspective."

Victor nodded. He understood what she wanted. He could have that by tomorrow afternoon.

FIVE

Tuesday Afternoon

Clarene stood in the center of the auditorium, her left foot tapping the floor impatiently. "Victor!" she called out for the third time. "Where are you?" She'd gotten off the phone a few minutes earlier and immediately began looking for him. His car was in the parking lot so she knew he had to be around the building somewhere.

"What?" he demanded testily, his voice coming from the hallway on the other side of the auditorium wall. The sound of the men's room door being slammed shut punctuated the air. A moment later his round frame burst around the corner into the auditorium. "Good God, Clarene, can't a guy go to the head without you interrupting? What is it? What's so important?"

"Janice called. She just got off work and is on her way over, wants to talk about her experience in class last night."

"I'll be happy to meet with her."

"She's coming to see me."

"Oh."

"Don't be upset Victor. Women like to talk to women about these type of things. She's concerned about what's going on. She wants to do more, but she also wants me to tell her its going to be all right. You know, give her assurances. It's all very new to her."

"And, that's why you were yelling for me? To tell me she's coming to see you…"

"No! That's not it at all. She'll be here shortly and…," she saw the look in his face, the lack of understanding. "Don't you see?" she said forcefully, "this is day five. This is my opportunity to learn what I can from her about why the dam is going to be blown up."

"I thought we agreed not to push her?"

"I'm not going to push her! She wants to talk. I want to listen. Come on, Victor, we're wasting time. She'll be here shortly. Before she gets here, I need to know what you found out for me about nineteenth century California."

"Quite a bit, actually," he said briskly, now that he understood why she wanted him. "I think you'll be pleased."

"Well, let's go to my office. I want to hear it."

Office was too strong a word for her room in the front corner of the building. Clarene used it primarily for psychic readings and only incidentally for Institute paperwork. It was large, sparingly furnished, and yet totally comfortable. When they arrived, the drapes were open and the afternoon light drifted through the large windows onto the white couch. Clarene gracefully eased her tall body onto the soft cushion on the right side.

Victor remained standing and pulled some folded paper from the inside pocket of his jacket. He flourished it dramatically into reading position with one hand as he pushed the round-framed bifocals back into position on his pudgy nose with the other. Looking to see he had her full attention, he began.

"California in the 1820's was owned by Spain and divided into two major areas: Baja and Alta. Mexico felt they should be in control of the land, but couldn't succeed since they were constantly in the throes of internal strife caused by the Spanish and the French. In 1821, Mexico finally threw Spain out and by May of 1822, Agustin de Inturbide had become President, then Emperor. In 1823, the Mexican Governor of Alta California, Arguella, signed an agreement with the Russians letting them hunt Otter from Cape San Lucas to the Port of San Francisco. At the same time, though, he began to expand the colonization of Alta California to prevent the Russians from getting a permanent foothold.

"A big factor of the times were the Mission Padres. They weren't trusted by the Mexicans because the Padres remained loyal to Spain, even after the Mexicans took over the Missions. The original plan had been to give the mission lands and holdings to the Indians, but that didn't happen. Instead, it was sold or given away as political rewards by the Governors. Since most of what the Indians produced was taken by the Padres for themselves, and nobody ever gave them enough food and clothing to survive, the Indians died off at the rate of two for every three born. By 1824 they were stealing horses to eat and had started revolts at a number of Missions.

"Things weren't too good in other parts of Alta California in 1824, either. The Russians were encroaching on San Francisco and for a while it looked like Spain – who hadn't given up their ownership – might cede all of Alta California away. The Mexicans and Spanish then got into a battle at Monterey and two Spanish warships surrendered to Arguella. To strengthen the Army against both the Russians and the Spaniards, Mexico sent convicts north as conscripts. As things got worse, a new territorial Governor, Colonel José Maria Echeandia, took over the Presidio in early 1825."

Victor paused, shuffling the papers. Clarene gave him a pleased look along with an affirmative shake of her reddish-topped head.

"That's kind of what I expected," she said. "It's a time of political turmoil and strife. Lot's of open spaces, nobody's really in control with lots of jockeying for position. Well, that's what I needed to know."

"Wait!" Victor held up his hand. "There's more. The good part is coming!"

Clarene raised her thin brown eyebrows, saw the 'have I got something for you' look in his eyes and settled herself back on the couch.

"In 1826, with matters not improving, the Mexicans sent a new Military Commandant, Ramon Felipe Garcia, to Monterey to take over the training and staffing of the Presidio. He brought his only daughter with him, a twenty-two year old, dark-eyed, black-haired beauty named Isadora Antonia-Maria."

Clarene listened intently.

"He had a lot of problems with her. She was constantly sick on board the ship from Mexico and then complained bitterly that life at the Presidio was not what she had been promised. In addition, the Officers there were little more than boys and certainly not a group from which a woman of her education and status would be able to chose a suitable husband.

"She found the food terrible, the fog from the Bay emotionally depressing and life at the Presidio full of dreary drudgery. She chastised her father daily about the conditions, as if somehow in his position as Military Commandant he could change them. The more she persisted, the more he was forced to console her. He finally got angry and decided to return her to Sonora, but the opportunity didn't come right away."

"How did you find all this?"

"It's based on his diary. I found the information in a story in **Early Days,** a historical magazine that covers the history of California. Anyway, after he promised to return Antonia-Maria to Sonora, she quieted down and life at the Presidio took on a more pleasant atmosphere, for awhile. Two ships came and left for Mexico without her, though, because she refused to spend another day at sea. Garcia tried to be understanding, but she was again causing him a lot of trouble. He prayed daily for help in sending her on her way.

"It wasn't long before the Lieutenant Governor, Jaime Ricardo Montefluelus, reached a point of despair with the situation after receiving far too many complaints from the other women at the

Presidio. He ordered Garcia to send Antonia-Maria back to Sonora by coach. Garcia began to make preparations, but became concerned about her protection during the journey. Montefluelus said if Garcia would take responsibility for getting her the first 200 miles from Monterey to San Ramon, he would guarantee her safety south from San Ramon to Sonora, using troops loyal to de Inturbide.

"Garcia, of course, didn't have a lot of choice in the matter. He also didn't have a lot of seasoned soldiers to choose from, nor spare, so he picked the best four among the convicts he'd been training. Montefluelus insisted that the coach leave by the first Monday in August and Garcia made plans for his daughter to be ready. It's interesting to note at this point, that the magazine article I got this from is entitled: *Antonia-Maria, Scapegoat or Heroine?*"

"Obviously something happened along the way. What?"

"That's the mystery. The coach never reached San Ramon and the four soldiers and the driver were never heard from again. There are few facts and a lot of speculation."

"Don't keep me in suspense." Clarene played with her words.

"Montefluelus's order to Garcia was a deception. The real reason for sending the coach south was to carry a wooden strongbox containing gold coins taken from the *Constante*, one of the Spanish ships that had surrendered to Arguella. There was also a leather pouch, for the personal attention of Presidente de Inturbide."

"Pouch? What was in it?"

"A map showing the location of a huge deposit of silver. The Mexicans found it in the Captain's cabin on the Constante. The Spanish had discovered the deposit but certainly didn't want the Mexicans to know about it. True to the spirit of the time, no one could be trusted and Arguella didn't tell anyone about the gold coins or the map when he was replaced as Governor by Echeandia. So it was a complete surprise when Montefluelus received orders to send the coins and the map to Sonora within weeks of Arguella's return to Mexico. Why Arguella didn't take them with him when he went back to Sonora, is part of the mystery. Anyway, Mexico was almost broke and needed the gold. The map, of course, could lead them to a secure future.

"Montefluelus wasn't happy about the idea of sending the gold or the map by ships that could be attacked by the Spanish and decided to send them, instead, by coach. He also decided the perfect cover was to force Antonia-Maria to leave, giving him the excuse to coerce Garcia into sending soldiers along. As the time approached for the coach to leave, Montefluelus had the local carpenter build a hiding place under the floor for the box and the pouch containing the map."

"Did Antonia-Maria's father know all of this?"

"Not in the beginning. As Lieutenant Governor, Montefluelus played by the rules of the times. He also had good reason for not telling Garcia what was on board, since the guards on the first leg of the trip were former convicts."

"Why didn't he insist on using some of the regular soldiers?"

"Garcia couldn't spare them. But more importantly, if Montefluelus had insisted on using regular soldiers, it would have brought undo attention to the coach."

"How did Garcia finally find out?"

"About a month after the coach left Monterey, news reached the Presidio that it had failed to arrive in San Ramon. Naturally, Garcia became quite distraught over the fate of Antonia-Maria. When he heard the whispers about the carpenter leaving the Presidio the day after the coach had departed, he concluded the youth had gone after his daughter and demanded that Montefluelus tell him what he knew about the man.

"Distraught himself over the loss of the gold and the map and seeking to share the blame that was coming his way, Montefluelus blurted everything to Garcia. Not only that, he blamed Garcia for sending convicts who probably deserted, instead of providing trained soldiers to protect the valuable shipment. Enraged, Garcia stormed out of the Presidio with a squad of his best soldiers and headed south, retracing the route taken by the coach. Three weeks later, he returned without having found the coach or Antonia-Maria. It was then that the rumors began. One said the gold jarred loose from its hiding place and when the convicts found it, they deserted leaving Antonia-Maria to a brutal end at the hands of the local Indians. Another rumor said Antonia-Maria and the guards fought fiercely to save themselves, but in the end were killed by the Indians, who then burned the coach in an arroyo, without ever seeing the gold. And yet another said the boxes were never put on the coach, but, instead, were hidden by the carpenter at the Presidio on the orders of Montefluelus, who wanted it all for himself. There were many rumors about the silver lode, too, and while many looked, no one ever found it. The map showing its location was never found either. The Spanish, of course, never acknowledged it existed and it quickly became known as *El Tesoro Fantasma*, the ghost lode."

"How poetic, Victor. Lost gold and a lost map to a silver lode. That's the stuff of legends; how come I haven't heard about it before?"

"I don't know. Neither had I. There was a lot of interest at the time, according to the magazine, but since no one ever found a trace of either the gold or the silver, things kinda waned. I'm sure if anyone today thought it was true, they'd start looking again."

"Probably. That's quite a tale," she said. "You really do enjoy delving into history, don't you?"

"Always have. I hope it helps you in your meeting with Janice."

"I'm sure it will. Thanks for the good work."

* * *

Janice sat at one end of the coach, her deep blue eyes focused on Clarene seated at the other end.

"Ever since last night," she said, "I haven't been able to put him out of my mind. I want to go back again, Clarene, it's like I'm being pushed from within. But, I'm scared, too. Will you help me when I try it again?"

"Sure I will," Clarene responded. "But, don't worry too much, it's very common for new students to feel a little fearful, especially in your case where you're dealing with a nightmare, as well."

"That's it, exactly. In my nightmares, I always panicked and tried to get off the horse. But, I didn't do that last night. If I go back again to that part and keep riding with him, maybe it will clear the nightmare. But at the same time, if something bad happens while I'm with him, I don't want to make a fool of myself in front of my classmates. Do you know what I mean?"

"Yes, I do. Perhaps you'd feel more comfortable in a private session."

"Could we? Let's do it now!" Janice twisted on the cushions, pulling her legs up under herself, bouncing with enthusiasm. Her eyes grew intense as her eyebrows arched up in anticipation. "Oh please, do. I don't want to wait."

"Well, we've got about an hour and a half before our Tuesday night classes start," replied Clarene. "Let me see if I can find Victor."

"Why do we need Victor? Can't we just do it by ourselves?"

"Not really. Victor's the expert in the field of past lives. He's the expert in getting people there and back and he's the expert in what to do when you're there. He knows the kind of guidance to give you and the questions to ask while you're in regression."

"You mean we can talk back and forth while I'm there?"

"Sure. You're not asleep and you're not dreaming. You're in a kind of self-hypnotic, deep meditation where your subconscious is more in control. You *can* hear and talk without disturbing your level of regression."

"I've been hypnotized before, in college," Janice said.

"You're probably a very good subject for hypnosis, then. No doubt that's why your first session went so well." Clarene stood up, holding out her hand to help Janice up. "You go on down to Classroom Four and get settled on a pad. Victor's in the library. I'll go get him. I'll just be a minute."

Janice walked straight down the hallway from Clarene's Office and entered the classroom. She picked the same pad and placed it on the soft, blue carpet in the same place as the night before. She had just removed her shoes and lain down when Clarene and Victor arrived.

"Hi, there, young lady," Victor greeted her enthusiastically, as he crouched down beside her. The growing bald on his head was clearly visible. "I'm pleased you want to try it again," he said, "Clarene will be right here to help, while I guide you through it."

Janice smiled.

"Well, then," he said, "let's begin."

He walked to the wall, dimmed the lights and softly began to intone his guiding words. She relaxed her entire body and followed as he led her once again through the forest to the lake. There, she saw herself reflected in the water and moments later, following a similar series of images to those of the previous evening, was again watching the young Mexican.

Victor sensed her regressed state. "Tell us what you see," he said.

Janice didn't respond right away, instead, allowing the scene to come into focus in her mind. "I'm on a horse, riding double with a bearded young Mexican. We're riding toward the foothills, dragging a wooden case behind us. Right now we're coming over a slight rise toward a riverbed. We…" Janice started to shake her head. Victor could see her body becoming taut.

"Don't concentrate on that right now," he quickly suggested in a soft voice. "Go back to where you were, before you got on the horse. Tell me what you see."

A moment passed and then, "I see a coach and two horses. The horses are dusty and look tired. Their heads are hanging down."

"What kind of coach is it?"

"Not too big. Short and boxy. Flat roof. A door on each side. Big wheels. A big leather cover and straps in back, probably for the baggage. A low, open seat for the driver in front. It might have been elegant once – but its paint is faded and the grayish wood underneath shows through."

"Where are you?"

"I don't know. It's bleak and barren. Dusty, dry adobe soil. A few trees scattered in the distance around a small building."

"Were you on that coach? Is that how you got there?"

"I think so." Janice got closer and looked inside. It was empty. She looked out the window on the far side toward where she had seen the small building, but, instead, saw rows of adobe huts come into view, with the ocean and a huge bay in the background.

"What do you see?" Victor asked quietly.

"I'm standing next to the coach, but now it's in front of a bunch of adobe huts. They're next to a big fort-like structure. Beyond that, there's a bay and the ocean. There's a ship in the bay, but it's not going anywhere, its sails are furled."

"All right, relax with that for a moment. Take it all in."

Victor looked at Clarene and they nodded at each other, knowingly.

"How are you observing the scene? Are you a participant?"

"I see things as though I am looking out from someone's eyes. I've gotten in the coach. I'm in a heavy reddish dress, much too hot for the day, but it insulates me from the winds coming off the bay. The tails of the horses are constantly swishing flies – they're everywhere. I smell the people standing around. Their odor is so strong…they must not have bathed for a long time. I can also smell the leather and wood in the coach." She paused. "A man in a blue and green uniform is standing next to the coach. He has a sword at his waist. His arm is through my window and his hand is resting on my shoulder. His face is sad."

"Is he saying anything?"

"He's speaking in Spanish. He has tears in his eyes and he keeps repeating the name Antonia-Maria. Oh! Another man just came up. He's in uniform, too, and is gently pulling the first man away. The coach is beginning to move. I see riders on either side, waving good-bye to the people near the huts. They are armed, two have lances, one has a small musket, but they are not dressed in uniforms."

"Do you know where you're going?"

"I feel like I am going home. I don't know where that is, but I feel happy about it."

"Take yourself deeper into the scene." Victor motioned to Clarene to turn the lights down to a mere dim. A moment later he saw Janice was completely relaxed on the pad, totally immersed in the scenes, becoming one with the woman in the coach.

She was happy to be leaving this wretched place! Her life as the Commandants daughter had been miserable and she was excited at going home! *Antonia-Maria*, she exclaimed to herself, *you are going home!* She adjusted her position on the hard seat and looked out the open window of the coach, watching the bay recede in the background.

She turned her thoughts to the journey to San Ramon and the smile changed to weary resolution as she remembered her father's admonitions – *Do not look at the soldiers or they will start to get ideas. Get out of the coach frequently and move about so sores do not develop on your backside. Take the water sparingly – only to slack your thirst between stops at campsites along the way. And, be prepared for a long journey, for while the horses are of sturdy stock, they will go no further than thirty miles a day. You cannot stay at the Missions along the way, for the Padres are loyal to Spain. We dare not tempt them to reveal your presence to the Spaniards. It will be better in San Ramon, where Inturbide's men will meet you.*

He had held her tightly as they left his quarters, kissing her often on the forehead as they walked. Helping her into the coach, he had whispered a final *vaya con dios* before putting his hand on her shoulder through the window.

The distance between the Presidio de Monterey and San Ramon was over 200 miles. If her father was right, it would take almost seven days for them to reach any form of real civilization again. Seven days in the coach would be forever, but when it was over, the rest of the journey to Sonora would be with real soldiers and Officers, in a real carriage. She stomped her foot, killing another of the interminable flies, but this time the floor gave off no hollow sound. She puzzled at that for a moment, but gave it no more thought as the coach bounced over yet another bump in the roadway.

"Are you all right?" Victor asked in a soft voice, touching Janice on the shoulder. "You're jerking."

"I was bouncing around in the coach, trying to find a comfortable position. Then I started to lose the image. Now I can't see the coach or myself. Everything's gone."

"All right, take your time," he said. "Relax. Come back slowly to this time and place. You are relaxed; your whole body feels refreshed. Slowly come back now…come back…come back. Blink your eyes." He waited. "Now open them."

Janice stretched, then sat up, wrapping her arms around her knees. She rested her chin on her kneecaps and looked at Clarene and Victor. "That was so real," she said.

"Yes," said Clarene, tenderly touching Janice's wrist. "You were telling us what you saw. Do you feel like standing?"

"I want to go back. Why didn't I go on?"

"Maybe you're not ready for all of it in one big session. Your mind probably wants to take it a step at a time, in bite-size segments."

"When can I go back? I want to see it all."

"Tomorrow night, if you feel up to it."

"Yes. Tomorrow, then. After work."

"We'll see. You might want to wait until after you've had a good night's sleep, before deciding."

Janice brushed her short, blond hair quickly into shape with her hands, adding vigor back to it after laying on the pad. After putting on her shoes, she slowly stood up, taking Clarene's hand for support.

"I'm sure I'll be back tomorrow. Promise me you'll be here," she said, hopefully.

"We'll be here. If you decide to wait until another day, that will be all right, too."

Janice nodded. She opened the classroom door and the sound of students talking and laughing in the social area down the hall reached her ears. Turning, she gave a little side-handed wave to Clarene and Victor and walked over to the front entrance. From there she walked slowly, deeply in thought, around the building to the parking lot and her car.

After Janice had gone, Victor turned to Clarene. "That was a good session," he said. "She'll be back tomorrow."

"I know. The way that past life of hers is trying to get out, nothing will keep her away."

"I'm amazed at what she's seen so far," he said. "She's got some very graphic images in her mind, doesn't she? For a beginner, she's doing very well, right up there with those students who have been with me for a long time. I'm very pleased for her."

"Yes. But it's taking time, Victor. This is Tuesday. I had the premonition last Thursday night. The death and destruction that are going to be caused by the dam being blown up is still going to happen – unless I can stop it! I have no doubt that Janice's Antonia-Maria is *your* dark-haired woman and I think the next session will tell us a lot more. But, I still don't know where the dam is, or why someone would want to blow it up! Each day it takes to find that out, is one less day for *me* to act. I know you're proud of what you've done with her in only two sessions and you should be. But in the real world," she said, emphatically stabbing the air in front of his chest with her finger, "I still don't know diddly-squat about how to stop it!"

"Perhaps I missed it," Victor snapped back sarcastically, "but I don't recall God appointing you General Manager of the world. And I sure as hell don't think he's going to hold you responsible if the dam blows up, in spite of your having tried to stop it!"

Clarene stared at him. "I had that dream for a reason, Mr. Alexander! And *I do have a responsibility* to try and stop it!" She faced him squarely, legs slightly apart for balance, hands on her hips, voice rising. "The problem is, you're not really interested, because you're not in command of stopping it."

"In command?" he retorted, moving to his left, to gain the center of the room. "In command of what, Ms. Davis? Your monumental ego? The real reason for your obsession about this dam is to try and gain what you can for your own purposes – to somehow save the Institute, to somehow put more money in your pocket because of the publicity you'd gain from stopping it from being blown up. I know you and your ego, Clarene! Saving the dam and all the people downstream is a wonderful, humanistic way to achieve your real purposes!"

"Damn you Victor! Damn you all to hell! You know very well *I always* think of others first!" She stood there glaring at him, daring him to say more, but not waiting. "There is a real disaster about to happen, but I can't run to my friends in the Sheriff's Department and say one's coming. They'd want the same details I'm looking for. *I know it's* going to happen and *you know* it's going to happen – unless one of us stops it. But, I don't see *you* trying to stop it, do I?"

Victor shook his head, involuntarily.

Emphatically pointing her finger at him again, she raised her voice. "Well, that leaves only me, buster!"

There was no doubt about her anger as she strode out of the room.

"Hey!" he shouted after her. "Don't get so upset! I was just trying to put things in perspective, to take the load off your shoulders." He tried smiling at her, but she had already turned the corner.

It didn't matter though, he knew she would need him tomorrow.

SIX

Wednesday Evening

Clarene ignored Victor throughout the day, purposefully avoiding the library whenever she came to the kitchen for tea. They'd had these spats before and she knew it was the best way to handle the situation. Nevertheless, she was concerned about his negative attitude and vowed to talk to him in a rational, unemotional way about it as soon as possible.

Her day had gone by quickly, filled with readings from nine in the morning until late into the afternoon. She had finished with her last client around five and was sitting on her couch, relaxing and recharging her energy, when Janice suddenly bounced through the doorway and greeted her with a boisterous, "Hey, there, you ready?"

Clarene jerked upright in startled reflex and then began laughing in unison with Janice as her infectious enthusiasm quickly filled the room.

"I found Victor in the Library," Janice added. "He's coming down the hall now, so let's do it!" She turned from the door and seeing Victor a step away, grabbed him by the arm and pulled him into Clarene's office. Still unable to contain herself, she grabbed Clarene's arm, too, and squeezing three-abreast, lead them down the hallway to start another session. It was 5:42 p.m.

Janice barely waited for Victor to turn the lights down before starting her own self-hypnotic process. With Victor intoning in the background, it took her only moments to reach a quiet level of deep contemplation, re-entering the coach as it continued to bump along. She was soon totally engrossed in the commotion.

Six days of this! My rump is very sore, Antonia-Maria thought, as she once again shifted, trying to find a comfortable position on the seat. Her temper was getting shorter with each mile.

"Stop the coach, I want to get out," she abruptly demanded. But the driver and the guards ignored her, as they had been doing lately in response to her increasingly frequent demands. It was obvious to her that the convicts had little desire to remain civil to her. She too, felt no bond with them, or the driver for that matter. The bonds that sometimes develop with a small group of travelers were certainly not evident here. On the contrary, she now felt concerned as the last semblance of civility disappeared and the guards talked openly about deserting and leaving her on her own.

Antonia-Maria was enraged! "I'm the Commandant's daughter," she screamed at them through the window. "He'll kill you if anything happens to me!"

But, they only laughed and taunted her more. By early afternoon they were threatening to remove her from the coach and satisfy themselves at her expense, before leaving her to die in the open while they fled to San Ramon.

Keep quiet, she told herself. *Ignore those wretched souls, they would not dare to harm me. Dios! How long will it be before we meet up with others?* But the miles went on without relief from the bouncing, jostling coach, or the taunts from the guards. Antonia-Maria began to pray for somebody to come along and take her away from it all.

Her mind began to drift, shaping the image of the man that would come to rescue her. He would be an Officer, of course. He would ride up and immediately realize her need. He would dispatch the convict-soldiers and take her away to San Ramon and then stay and protect her all the way to Sonora.

It was late afternoon when the coach and riders reached the Los Robles Valley, little more than a long day's ride from San Ramon.

That night, she stayed in the campsite only to eat, then walked far outside the circle of light to lie down on her blanket, firmly holding in her right fist the thin knife her father had given her. She got little sleep that night, constantly worried about an assault that never came.

But, the next morning it became clear the guards had set their plans. She heard them brazenly talking of the things they would do to her and realized this could be her last day on earth. She desperately looked for a means of escape, but found none and was forced to listen in terror as they described how they would seize her at the next rest stop, then enjoy their pleasures before stealing fresh horses for the ride into San Ramon. Fear grasped and knotted her stomach as her mind raced faster, seeking an escape, yet unwilling to give up the immediate security of the coach and the driver. *The driver!* she thought. *He'll help me! He hasn't been part of their plans!*

"She's trembling, Clarene," Victor exclaimed, concerned. "She's really trembling. I want to bring her back."

"Let her go on, Victor. Help her."

"Janice," he said with the soft, firm voice he always used in class. "Don't become fully involved. You are watching something that happened a long time ago. Become an observer rather than a participant. You are there to learn, you don't have to relive any pain."

Janice subconsciously nodded her head, but at the same time was drawn more firmly into the scene before her eyes as she continued with her running dialog and descriptions.

"I just heard the guards say they had seen someone coming.

The coach is picking up speed and we are bouncing wildly over hard ground with lots of small rocks."

To Antonia-Maria, their hurried talk and gestures indicated the driver and the guards didn't want to take any chances. She tried to see who was coming, but could not get a clear view from where she sat inside the swaying coach. Using its heaving and jolting, she bounced across the seat to the opposite window and looked out to see a rider, framed by the blue of the cloudless sky, bearing down on them at a full gallop.

Dios mio, you do answer prayers! she cried out as she crossed herself. Leaning her head through the open window, she eagerly tried to get a closer look at her rescuer. As he came into closer view, she was devastated to see that the dark-haired, bearded young man waving his sweat-stained leather hat in the air wore no uniform and had no sword. Worse yet, he was calling out to the convict-soldiers, by name!

Dejected, she slumped back into the hard seat and started to cry.

The coach slowed as the driver and the soldiers recognized Carlos, the carpenter from Monterey. When it stopped, the swirling dust caught up from behind and enveloped them all for a moment before passing on.

As the air cleared, Carlos called out to the driver. "I have a message for you from the Lieutenant Governor." He reined his horse in, easily slipping off the saddle as the animal came to a halt next to the coach. Antonia-Maria watched as the convict-soldiers rode up, approaching cautiously.

"There is a change in your destination," he said, impassively. "There has been a revolt by the Mission Indians in San Ramon. It is not safe to travel near there now. Montefluelus received word of it the day after you left, from the Captain of a newly-arrived ship."

"Why did they send *you* to tell us?" asked the driver, suspiciously. "Why didn't Montefluelus send a troop of soldiers?"

"He could not spare them. I once lived in San Ramon and

know this valley. I told him I would catch up to you and stop you before you started over the mountains. We must go to the Mission Santa Delores at Los Robles and wait until we receive word it is safe to proceed. It's only a few miles from here. We can follow the riverbed over there." He pointed to the west.

The convict-soldiers stared in disbelief at the carpenter as they heard the news. Inside the coach, Antonia-Maria found new breath as she saw an opportunity to escape her fate. She climbed out, but the door brushed against one of the soldiers as it swung open. Startled, he jerked back, quickly saw what she was doing and, with anger in his eyes, aggressively yelled at her to "Get back in there."

The other three guards moved towards her as well, anger burning on their faces. One grabbed her by her wrist and pushed her up against the coach as the others surrounded her. She tried to keep her balance and get away from them, but stumbled instead, and fell to the ground.

The driver immediately jumped off the coach and pushed his way past the soldiers to help her up. His reward was to be clubbed on the head with a lance, dropping him to the ground beside her.

"Hold them," shouted the tallest of the guards, running toward the backside of the coach. He returned shortly holding some leather strips he had cut from the baggage straps. As he reached down to tie Antonia-Maria's hands he was startled to see the carpenter pointing a brace of pistols at him and the others.

"What is this?" the guard demanded. "Let us be with her. This is nothing to you. You have delivered your message – now go!"

Carlos did not move. Instead, he continued to point the pistols at them, looking particularly menacingly at the tall one. Slowly, but adamantly, he said, "Put your lances and knives on the ground, under the coach. If any of you have a pistol, do the same. Then start running for the rest stop. It's not that far."

When they did not comply, he shouted at them. "Do it, or I will kill you!"

The tall one did not comprehend and tried to put Carlos at ease. "If you want her, you can have her first. We just want her, too."

"Go!" Carlos barked the command, pointing a pistol directly at him.

The guard looked quizzically at the carpenter, then decided to do as he was told and placed his weapon under the coach. He nodded at the other three, who followed his lead, carefully placing their weapons on the ground under the coach, too. Together, they backed away slowly until they were even with the horses. There they hesitated.

"*¡Andale!* Run now!" Anger rose in Carlos' voice. "*¡Andale! ¡Andale, pronto!*"

They started walking again, slowly backwards, knowing full well that each pistol held but one shot and there were four of them. Yet, none chose to be the first or second to die and they continued to retreat, backing away from the menacing pistols.

Antonia-Maria knew she had been saved and started to get up to thank her savior, but the driver intervened, holding up his hand in warning. She turned to see the pistols were now pointed at them.

"Go anywhere you want," Carlos said. "But, leave!"

Anger and fear welled up inside her. Outraged at the man for betraying his obligation to rescue her, she abruptly stood up and in two steps, tried to reach out and slap the insolent carpenter. Again, the driver saved her.

Ignoring them both for a moment, Carlos glanced at the four guards and saw they were now a good distance from the coach. Turning back, he started towards the coach, but his way was blocked by Antonia-Maria and the driver. Frowning at their still being there, he jerked his head in a get-out-of-the-way motion that was unmistakable and frightening. The two quickly moved away from his path.

He flung the door open, then pushed and pulled on the floorboard in a peculiar manner until it came loose, revealing the opening he had constructed, and the box inside. He jerked on the box to remove it, but his awkward efforts did not succeed; it was stuck. Anger rising, he jumped inside the coach and, using his legs for leverage, shoved it free. Lifting it out, he slid the box away on the floor and then started feeling around under the floorboards for the pouch. It too, had become lodged over many days of the rough ride, but, with determination, he soon had it free.

Antonia-Maria and the driver had stopped moving away from the coach as soon as Carlos began to remove the box. They now watched closely, curiosity rising and edging nearer as he dragged it through the door and dropped it to the ground. In the distance, the guards became curious, too.

Concentrating on his task, Carlos looped his rope around and over the box several times, tying it securely. As he did, Antonia-Maria glanced over her shoulder and saw the tall guard suddenly start running toward the distracted carpenter. As she watched, the other three guards began running toward the coach, as well.

Oblivious to the running men, the driver sought to get a better view and inadvertently placed himself directly in the path of the on-rushing tall guard. As they collided, each grabbed the other in desperate reaction. Staggering from the impact, they stumbled for a few steps before falling together to the ground.

Carlos jerked around, grabbed his pistols and pointed them menacingly at the two men, then at the three other guards who quickly stopped abreast of the horses.

Satisfied they would not act stupidly again, he put the pistols in his waistband, tied the loose end of the rope to his saddle horn and stuffed the leather pouch into his saddlebag. Without delay, he mounted his reddish-brown mustang and began to flee.

"Take me with you!" Antonia-Maria screamed. "They mean to kill me. You must take me with you!"

But he had already reined the horse away and her heart dropped. All was lost! She started to collapse, but seconds later he wheeled back, grabbed her around the waist and pulled her awkwardly onto the horse and over the rope trailing behind him. He sunk his spurs into the belly of the scraggly, hairy-legged animal and it lunged forward, galloping off toward San Ramon. The rope chafed viciously at the inside of her leg as the wooden strongbox skipped and bounced across the hard adobe clay behind them. She desperately held onto his waist, trying to catch her breath.

Once out of sight of the coach, they slowed as Carlos guided the horse over the edge of a small arroyo, down to a dry riverbed. Antonia-Maria's eyes remained closed, her arms tightly grasped around his waist. *God did answer prayers!* she thought. This *man knows what he is doing. I'll stay with him!*

Moments later the horse stopped and Carlos jumped off. Leading it by the reins, he looked around, searching.

"Thank you for saving me," she said, watching him from the saddle. "My father will reward you for this."

"Your father would kill me for this. That's why I took you. If they catch me, the soldiers from the Presidio at San Ramon may be willing to bargain for you."

"How would the soldiers find us so quickly?"

"They roam this valley looking for Indians and stolen horses. They will find the coach and the guards, then they will come looking for us."

"Why did we stop? Why don't we continue to run?"

"Because that wooden box will soon fall apart. The sounds of the wood tell me it won't hold together much longer. I'm going to hide it for now."

"What's in it?"

"Gold, I think."

"My father said nothing about gold."

Su padre jugaron una mala pasada – y usted, también. "They played a dirty trick on your father – and you, too."

"*Maldito!*" Perturbed at the revelation, she abruptly got off the horse and joined him, wanting to be near his strength and to help, if she could. They had walked a short distance and were at a bend in the riverbed, when he looked up, startled, listening intently.

She heard it, too. From far behind them came the soft rumblings of many hooves against the hard clay. There were so many, they could feel the ground begin to vibrate. He quickly led the horse to his intended hiding place – a small cave with a narrow entrance, a few feet up from the edge of the riverbed.

He took the pouch from the saddlebag and shoved it inside his shirt, then untied the rope from the saddle horn and began dragging the box toward the entrance. She grabbed the rope too, trying to help in spite of being hampered by her heavy skirt. The mustang suddenly bolted and ran. She started to go after it, but he pulled her down and shoved her forward on her hands and knees into the entrance. Once inside, she found it large enough to turn around. She grasped and helped pull the box in while he continued to push until it was fully inside the cave. He crawled in beside her, then twisted around to face the entrance, pistols at the ready. It had taken them less than a minute, but his breathing was so heavy she feared it would give them away.

Seconds later she realized the vibrations and noise had stopped, replaced by a strange quiet. She immediately feared the soldiers were nearby.

"Maybe they'll follow the horse," she said in his ear. He nodded, his silhouette clearly outlined to her by the light coming through the entrance to the small cave.

"Do you see them? Are they there?" she whispered, desperately.

He shook his head as he peered out the entrance. He suddenly jerked back in fright as the ground began to vibrate again, quickly escalating into a violent lurching that terrified them both. From outside the cave they could hear the monstrous groaning and ripping of earth being torn apart. He instantly realized he had chosen the wrong place to face the wrong enemy!

Antonia-Maria knew it, too, and kicked at him. "It's an earthquake!" she screamed. "Get out. Get out!"

He tried to move, but the entrance collapsed, blocking his way and the light. Even as they both squirmed toward the darkened exit, the ground shuddered more and more violently, spewing dust all over them. Antonia-Maria choked, coughing in spasms as the ceiling began to disintegrate, covering them with clods of dirt and rock. She was terrified and grabbed for his hand, squeezing it in dread. He held her tightly in return, his eyes seeking hers in vain.

Abruptly, the roof collapsed, dropping its load of boulders and dirt over their bodies, pinning them in the darkness.

It was over.

SEVEN

Wednesday Evening

Janice clawed wildly at the air with her hands and desperately kicked her legs, as whimpers of terror stifled in her throat. Seconds later, she lay limply on her pad, breathing in deep spasms as the images of Antonia-Maria's smothered end became obliterated in the darkness of a past century. Clarene quickly layed down next to her, cuddling her in comforting compassion.

Victor kneeled down on the other side of Janice and gently, soothingly began to talk her back to the present. It took a few moments for his voice to penetrate the veil, but when it did, she responded to his commands and slowly eased herself away from her subconscious journey. He methodically persisted, talking her back to the present cautiously, deliberately.

She finally blinked her eyes and looked around the room. When she saw Clarene, she grabbed her tightly and began to sob, then bawl. Within moments she was gasping for air amidst tempered shrieks.

Victor tried, but couldn't calm her down with his soothing words. As Janice continued out of control, he looked at Clarene and asked in a pleadingly voice, "What can I do? I don't know how to stop her."

"She doesn't need to stop," Clarene stated. "This has been in her system for almost 200 years. It's time it got out so she can get on with life. Let her go. She'll be all right."

"But she's crying so much…so hard. She'll…"

"Let it be, Victor! Why is it you men never understand the value of crying? It's necessary and it's therapeutic. If the crying bothers you, leave! I'll watch her. She'll be all right!"

"I just feel badly at the way things turned out. I just never expected her to face an end like that."

"Neither did I. Neither did she." Clarene reached out to touch his hand. "I know her crying is upsetting to you, but look at the positive side – you were successful in helping her reach a drama in a past life that was causing her problems in this one. With your guidance, she came face to face with her fear of being smothered by men. Now she knows why and can deal with it. That's what this is all about, Victor. Be pleased with yourself."

"If you say so." He looked down at Janice and then back up to Clarene. "I appreciate the kind words, thanks."

Clarene looked at her watch. "It's close to seven. Go down to the social room and stall your students for a few minutes, will you? I'll try and get Janice up and take her to my class. It'll do her good."

As Victor left, Clarene gave Janice a long, tight hug, then released her and said, tenderly, but firmly, "That's enough crying now. You came to learn about yourself and you did. It's been a terrifying experience, but treat it for what it is, something that happened in another time, in another place. You're here with *me* now, in this room and you're alive. Put it into perspective."

Clarene stood up and held out a hand. "I've got an Introduction class to conduct. Why don't you join us? It'll do you good."

Janice pulled herself up and followed Clarene, somewhat unsteadily, down the hall to Classroom One, near the front entry. She sat down in one of the comfortable, cushioned chairs at the rear of the room and waited as the other students began to filter in.

She watched through glazed eyes as the room filled. Even though she tried to keep alert to what Clarene was saying, Janice began to relive the terror that had come to her inside the cave. Aware that some students were watching her, she fought to subdue and control her visible emotions, even though the scenes relentlessly swirled around in her mind.

Forcing herself to focus on Clarene, she saw her at the whiteboard at the front of the room speaking to the class.

"This is our basic, introductory course. Here, you'll learn about yourself. We will teach you how to like, maybe even love yourself, in a non-egotistical way. We will teach you how to take control of your life, so you can become the person you want to be. At the same time, we will teach you about anger, hate and jealousy and how to deal them, both in yourself and in others. Best of all, we'll give you an overall introduction to New Age concepts and let you decide what to pursue in more depth, later.

"To some, this is a whole new world and every step must be examined. To others, it's a return to knowledge, whether gained in this lifetime or another. Such students usually accelerate rapidly. The main thing for you to remember is this: it is not a race! At this time *and at any other time in your life,* you will always be exactly where you need to be! That's a profound statement that may take you some time to understand. Nevertheless, in the long run, you'll come to know it's true."

She looked around the class, gaining eye contact with individual students. "Don't look to others for validation," Clarene went on. "Give it to yourself, instead. Do things for yourself. Don't sell your soul to someone because they tell you what you want to hear. You will always bring onto yourself that which you need to learn in this lifetime. In many cases it means releasing something from your past, whether in this lifetime or another. Anger at the way an old lover dropped you, being upset with your parents or a trusted friend, the return of an old nemesis, are a few examples of situations you may run into. Learn from the experience, release your attachment to it and get on with life as quickly as possible. In other words, don't pack old karma around with you like a ball and chain."

Janice thought of Carlos, visualizing him as a ball and chain clamped to her ankle.

* * *

After class, Clarene offered to drive Janice home, but she declined. She would be all right, she insisted, as Clarene walked her to the Camero.

After watching her leave the parking lot, Clarene returned inside and said her goodnights to the other students before quietly leaving to go to her own home. She was mentally exhausted and longed for the quiet comfort of her bed.

A short time later, she sat comfortably in her nightgown at the edge of her queen-sized bed, sipping Frangelica and letting her mind drift where it might. As she looked around the room, focusing on nothing in particular, a small river flowing from the mountains began to take form in her mind. Leaning back on her pillow, she followed the image, as it became a pleasant scene of gently flowing water. As she watched, though, it soon began to back up behind a dam. The body of water continued to grow, wider and longer, backing and filling until a huge lake had formed behind the dam. As she continued to watch, the water of the lake began to churn, thrusting itself again and again against the dam's three giant gates, trying to get free. Suddenly the gates sprang open, unleashing the mass.

Absorbed with the captivating scene, Clarene saw the water churn forth over the spillways, rush down the old, dry riverbed and then slam into a ranch, destroying the house and all else in its path. Drawn by the tragedy once again playing in her mind, the spectacle of the powerful, rushing water grabbed her and plunged her rapidly and deeply into a trance-like state. Once there, the next chapter in her premonition began to unfold, its terrifying reality abetted this time by compelling and fantastically distorted images.

The water immediately took on the form of a cunningly invincible entity. Long held back from its natural journey to the sea, it was now free to concentrate its energies on any obstructions that lay in its rightful path.

Once past the ranch, the huge wall of water careened west through the valley, overflowing the boundaries of the old riverbed. As it hurtled forward, it pounded into a deep arroyo and abruptly found itself being forced into a sharp turn to the left by a curving, fifteen foot high wall of clay and rock that somehow looked like a miniature half-dome. The maelstrom briefly fought against the restraint, but upon sensing the concrete two-lane bridge less than a half mile away, began to prepare itself, instead, for the task ahead. The earth groaned as the lead wave smashed into the curve, throwing water high into the air as the boiling, frothing mass awkwardly ricocheted southward, quickly regaining its momentum.

The steel gate, robbed of its once stately dignity, careened toward the curve at full force. Sensing that it would need something strong and unyielding to use as a cutting blade on the bridge, the headlong rush of turbulence maneuvered the massive gate into a clump of sturdy branches eager to grasp and hold it. As it reached the curve, one of the huge limbs skewed around in the turbulent water and jammed its broken end into the muddy wall. Thus anchored, it forced the gate to swing effortlessly through the curve, turning it south with the flowing torrent. Then, just as quickly, by tenaciously hanging onto its charge, the limb was pulled free of the wall, enabling it to rejoin the mighty mass.

The churning water, continually reinforced by the emptying reservoir behind it, surged forth, adding boulders and trees to its sinew as it bore down on its' intended victim. Gathering pressure as the walls compressed it more tightly, the swirling torrent twisted and turned the steel gate into assault position, high and sideways in a royal throne of oak. Before it would be used though, the leading edge of water would hit and clear the approaches to the bridge.

Clarene was terrified to see a car approaching from the east, speeding toward its destiny. Throwing her hands up in wild, panic motions, she screamed at it to STOP! To TURN! To GO BACK!

The driver ignored her.

Jerry McCormick knew the valley; had driven it many times, was familiar with all of it's curves and hills and was in a hurry to get to his uncle's ranch in Los Robles. He'd been driving all night and was eager to be there in time for breakfast. He had been holding the SUV at a steady seventy for some time now, but since he knew he was approaching a narrow bridge and a curvy section of road ahead, he decided to slow down a bit.

Smiling at the sleeping form of his wife, Joanna, in the right front seat, he pushed the controls on his door to open both side windows slightly to start waking her up. Sunlight crept through the mountains behind him and the wind whipped through the windows, striking him on the back of the head. The wind seemed to bear a roaring noise to his ears, but it wasn't loud enough to recognize or be of concern.

The coming drama now took shape, as Clarene watched, horrified at the grotesque images the water was forming in her mind.

Sensing greater prey, the plunging, tormented mass sent its scouts splashing high into the air to report. Then, using the unremitting force feeding it from behind, the leading edge tossed its head one last time, picked up a little speed, then hunkered down, close to the riverbed, readying itself to clear the approaches to the two concrete pilings that supported the bridge.

The roar of the oncoming water again reached Jerry's ears, but he still suspected nothing as the whistling of the wind around the windows continued to mislead him. As the car zipped through the last turn, the water, frothing through the air, caught his eye. Bewildered by the sight, he took his foot off the accelerator and the car promptly slowed. In that instant, he heard the water's full roar and saw the disastrous rendezvous ahead. If he had acted instantly, he might have swung the big SUV around, avoiding his fate. Instead, he slammed on the brakes and it skidded forward to the center of the bridge, where it nosed to a halt, engine dead.

The ugly mass of water quickly cleared any lingering rocks and debris from the underside of the bridge, as the main body drew on its concentrated energy, getting ready to slam the oak-throned steel gate into the pilings. Its roar smothered the sounds of Jerry's foot stamping on the accelerator and the grinding of the overworked starter, helplessly turning a flooded engine.

Jerry watched in terror as the hurtling gate careened towards the bridge, He screamed for Joanna to get out of the car and run! Run! Run! But Joanna couldn't move. She lay crumpled under the dash, where she had been thrown in the violent stop, dazed and oblivious to her fate. He might have saved himself, but love and fear held him fast.

The end of the branch holding the gate once again thrust forward, this time into the dirt at the edge of the concrete abutment joining the bridge to the riverbed. There it stayed long enough to whip the gate at an angle across the two pillars, knocking them down like bowling pins. The bridge collapsed into the inky, frothing mass with a loud cracking noise that was soon suffocated by the pandemonium of the triumphant water.

The tree branch released the gate and swiftly searched for a replacement. It soon found the SUV and grasped it firmly, carrying it onward toward the sea.

Before it reached that goal though, there was the village of Los Robles.

* * *

Clarene shuddered awake, trying to clear the malevolent, disastrously violent scenes from her mind. The overwhelming doses of fantasy and symbolism that the water had taken in the dream left her shaking and tormented.

Covered in perspiration, she flinched as she sat up in bed and saw that her sheets and blanket were in a pile on the floor, her cordial of Frangelica spilled on the nightstand beside her.

No need to try and remember the details of this dream, she thought. *How could I forget it? Water with a mind of its own, reaching out for the sea? This is getting bizarre! Has this thing gotten worse, to get my attention? Well let me tell you, dream, you have my attention! I'm going to find Los Robles and go there. Then I'm going to find that damn dam and do something about it!*

EIGHT

Thursday

"I've found it, Victor!" Clarene shouted excitedly into the telephone. "I've found the dam!"

"How? Where is it?" he shouted back, equally excited at hearing the news, even if it was seven in the morning.

"I had another dream last night. God, you wouldn't believe the things that went on in that dream! The water was heading for Los Robles, so this morning I looked it up on the map. Los Robles is where Mission Santa Delores is located – you know, the one Janice mentioned when she was regressed. It's on the other side of the mountains from San Ramon. It's all starting to come together!"

"But, what about the dam, Clarene? You said you found the dam."

"That's the point, Victor. When I was looking at the map, I saw a blue area for a lake, just east of Los Robles. And, you know what created that lake? The Los Vaqueros Dam, that's what! It's got to be the one. I've found it!"

"It sure sounds like it. Now what?"

"Oh, Victor, the first thing I have to do is calm down a bit and think things through. Then, I'm going to take a shower. Meet me at the Institute in an hour, will you?"

"You can't get ready in an hour, Clarene," he chided. "You know it takes you at least forty-five minutes just to do your hair. When you add all the other fruffing you do, you'll be lucky to eat and be there by nine. I'll see you then." He calmly but quickly hung up, pleased with her success, but not wanting to have his morning taken up with a long rebuttal about her ability to get ready in a hurry.

It was mid-morning when she finally arrived, dressed in tight fitting, green gabardine slacks and a white blouse. In her exuberance, she ignored her lateness and instead, promptly treated Victor to the whole panorama of her second dream. Then, she told him of her plans, conceived in the shower and solidified on the way to the Institute. He was astonished and concerned.

"You're going to take Janice with you? Why? Why involve her? After the darkness of the cave, there's nothing more she can contribute." He pushed his glasses back up his pudgy nose so he could look directly at her. "You'll be putting a lot of stress on her, for nothing."

"Calm down, Victor. She's going along to keep me company. The real purpose of the trip is for *me* to go to the dam. I'm sure it's going to be the same one I saw in my dreams. When I've confirmed that, I'll go to Bill Edwards and get the Sheriff involved. After all, we now have a motive – the gold and the map, buried in the cave."

Victor nodded; he'd come to that conclusion, too.

"By getting close to the dam, I may be able to pick up something I can use. Bill can't ask for the resources of the Sheriff's department just on my say-so. He'll need details to convince his boss. That's what I need to get – enough information about those involved to convince the Sheriff to move."

"What if you don't sense anything? Then what?"

Clarene shook her head. "It's got to be there. I have to find it! The pressure is building and I feel my time is running out. We've found the young woman you predicted, now I have to find the old man."

"Plenty of time for a person with your capabilities," he stated, softly.

"Don't start with the sarcasm, Victor," she responded. "This is very real to me."

"Hey! I really meant that. This thing is real for me, too — except for your last dream. I don't recall anything like that before. Malevolent, raging water, with an apparent mind of its own, purposefully destroying a bridge and a Sports Utility Vehicle for practice before taking on a whole town." He shook his head in rapid, little motions; "It's absurd."

"You're right. But that's the way the dream happened." She looked at him intently for a moment before continuing. "Back to your comment about Janice. *I did* think about the affect the trip might have on her, but I also think we owe it to her, to let her validate her past life experience. She's going to want to do that for herself sometime — it may as well be now, when I can be there with her. Besides, I want to hear any spontaneous comments she might make when she gets into that setting, maybe things we haven't heard before."

"Are you going to try and find the cave?"

"Probably not. There's so little to go on regarding its location. Carlos ordered the guards to go west to the Mission at Los Robles, but then he took Antonia-Maria in the opposite direction. How far he went is pretty hard to determine. Maybe something will trigger her when we're driving through the area. If so, I'll stop for her sake."

"It'll be a long drive. When are you going?"

"I expect Janice to come back this evening. I'll talk to her about it then. If she agrees, we'll leave tomorrow morning."

"I'd like to come along if I could, to help out."

"Thanks, Victor," she said, reaching out to touch his powerful, but stubby hands across the table. The gold bracelets on her tanned arm jingled in unison. "I appreciate the offer, but I'd rather go with Janice by myself. I'll tell you all about it when I get back."

"You're sure?"

"Yes. No offense intended."

"None taken. But, I am disappointed. I've gotten hooked on this thing and while I've been negative at times, I'm eager now to get involved."

"I know." Clarene patted his hand. "And, I *will* keep you involved. But this a girl thing. Let me have my time with her, alone. You stay here and keep writing, you need to finish that book."

He knew there was no arguing with her once her mind was made up. He smiled, got up, straightened his tie and jacket, and walked slowly to the library.

Clarene watched him leave, then started to get up. She quickly settled back into the chair, though, as she slipped into scenes from her dream, easily visualizing the viciousness of the rampaging water as it hurtled downstream. *Is Victor right,* she thought, *is it practicing? And, is Los Robles going to be its next victim? This is insane, water is just water; it can't acquire a personality. Why am I dreaming it has?*

The white phone on the pale pink wall to the right of the kitchen pass-through jangled twice before she got up.

"This is Clarene," she answered.

"Can I come over? Can we talk?" It was Janice. "I couldn't go to work today."

"I'm sure I've got nothing after three," Clarene answered, taking a moment to judge the tone in Janice's voice. "Would that be all right?"

"Yes," she replied, somewhat quietly.

"Are you all right?" Clarene asked, concerned.

"I think so, but I'm not sure."

"Do you want to come in now? I can cancel my appointments."

"No. I'll wait until three." Her voice was low, unemphatic.

A moment passed and she finished the call.

* * *

Five hours later Janice was again seated on the white couch in Clarene's office. She was dressed in clean, but old, bluejeans; legs curled up beside her, with her sandals dropped on the floor.

Clarene got up from behind her desk and walked over to join her, bracelets dropping down to her wrists as she moved. She kicked off her low-heeled white shoes and sat down. "How are you feeling?" she asked, "Did you get any sleep at all, last night?"

"Not much," said Janice. "I couldn't stop reliving the whole incident. Even when I'd fall asleep, I'd start dreaming about it. It got to the point I couldn't separate my dreams from that horrid past life. I was so exhausted this morning, I didn't go to work. I woke up late and then only long enough to call you. I finally got up and dressed a couple of hours ago."

"That was a rough experience, my friend. Not many people come face to face with that kind of an ending to a life. Do you want to talk it out?"

"It seemed so real yesterday when I was regressed, but now, after reliving it a thousand times, I'm not sure what's real, anymore."

"Would you like to corroborate it? Not the end, but the other parts? You know, to confirm the experience?"

"What do you mean? How would we do that?" Janice looked concerned.

"I'm not trying to scare you, Janice," Clarene said in consoling voice. "But I think it's important to put the whole experience into perspective. You need to know whether there's truth to the matter or not. Otherwise, you won't be able to handle it when it comes up again in your dreams – and it will."

Clarene watched Janice to see if the words were getting through.

"You remember what I said in class last night? This is something you have to face and put away in its proper place. It mustn't be able to face you down and control you. You can't let that happen. The best way to do that is to accept it, learn the lessons from it, and get on with your life!"

Janice started to feel a glimmer of hope that Clarene might be right. "I guess I'd like that, but I don't know how to do it. Where do I start?"

"We could start from where you were at the time the coach was stopped by Carlos and take it from there."

"But, how would we find that place? I don't know where it is; or was, I guess I should say."

"I do. Mission Santa Delores, where he ordered the guards to go, is near Los Robles. It still exists – it's on the other side of the mountains from San Ramon. We can start in that area. What do you think, do you want to go?"

"Yes." Her mind was already pulling up images of the coach and the guards as they bumped along toward the rest stop. She knew what to look for, if she got to the right place. "Can we go tomorrow?" she asked eagerly. "I'll take another day off. I'll even pack a picnic lunch."

Clarene was pleased with the enthusiasm. "Sure. I'll drive."

"How long will it take?"

"About two hours to get to San Ramon. Then another half-hour or so to Los Robles. If we leave around nine, we can be there before noon."

"I'll meet you here."

"It can get hot up there and we may be walking in areas with lots of dirt and rocks. Dress accordingly."

"OK. This is a great idea. Thanks."

Clarene smiled. "Good, glad you like it."

Janice suddenly remembered a question she wanted to ask. "Are those sessions ever taped? I mean, did you or Victor happen to tape my past life session last night, so I could listen to it?"

"Victor may have," Clarene answered. "He keeps a recorder in the classroom for that reason. I didn't see him do it, but then, again, I was concentrating on you. If he did, the tape should still be in the machine. Come-on, let's look."

Clarene lead the way from her office to Classroom Four and entered the room. She walked directly to the small table near the side wall and popped the lid on the tape recorder.

"Nothing here," she said, looking at the empty space. "If he did tape it, it would be here – unless he took it with him. Let's see if we can find him."

Janice followed Clarene again, this time to the library. Victor was not there, nor in the kitchen. "I know he was here," exclaimed Clarene. "I talked to him this morning and then saw him going into the library around noon." She hesitated for a moment. "I'll ask him about it when I see him."

"You don't suppose he put it someplace around here, do you?" Janice pleaded. "I'd sure like to hear it at home tonight, before we go tomorrow."

"I understand," Clarene replied. "If there is a tape, maybe he's got it with him for safekeeping. Right now, there's not much we can do. As I said, I'll ask him when I see him."

In spite of her outward calmness, Clarene was concerned, for it was obvious to her psychic side that there *was* a tape. But, if so, why hadn't Victor said so this morning? It was odd and it bothered her. She thought of calling him at home, but decided against it. In all the previous years she had worked with him, she had never called him at home. Now, in the last week, it was becoming a habit.

Clarene saw that Janice was downcast again. "Don't look so sad," she said. "If there is a tape, we'll get it. In the meantime, I think you're going to be all right. Go home and get something to eat and a good night's sleep. We're going to have a big day tomorrow."

Clarene walked with Janice to the parking lot, where they said their good-byes. As Clarene watched Janice drive away, she was surprised to see Bill Edward's green, four-wheel drive Blazer parked in the lot. She hadn't seen him inside.

NINE

Friday

Janice was already in the parking lot when Clarene arrived.

"Good heavens, Ja-neece, you're so prompt," she called out, as she got out her El Dorado. It was jet black, a classic '92 with a minimum of chrome. "Have you been here long?"

"Gosh no," replied Janice, walking over. "Only a few minutes. Well...maybe ten. I didn't want to keep you waiting." She grimaced and regretted the words; Clarene was a psychic and would know better. "Actually, I couldn't wait to get here, I've been excited all night."

Clarene chuckled. "Good. I'm glad you are. I see you're dressed for the adventure. Nice boots, too. Are they new?"

"No," she replied, looking down at the light brown cowboy boots she was wearing. "I've had them for a while. My friend, Teri, talked me into taking western dance lessons with her. I got this at the same time," she added, pointing to the blue and white patterned western shirt tucked inside her jeans. "We went dancing twice, then she met a guy and that was the end of the lessons. Now I wear the outfit on weekends. I hope it's all right."

"It's just fine, Ja-neece. The whole outfit looks good on you.

A lot better than mine does," she said, displaying her own boots, loose fitting casual jeans, and a summer-weight light pink shell. She didn't wait for the obligatory contradiction. "Got your picnic basket?" she asked.

"It's in the car. I'll get it." Janice answered.

"OK. Let me open my trunk."

Janice walked to her Camero and retrieved the small basket and transferred it to the Cadillac.

"Hope you have plenty of cold drinks in there," Clarene said. "I'm sure it's going to be hot up there. It's warm down here already."

"I've got a big jug of lemonade loaded with ice. I've also got some sandwiches and chips."

Clarene nodded with satisfaction, closed the trunk and got in the driver's side. Janice walked around and opened the door, then settled onto the smooth, dark brown leather of the passenger seat. Moments later they drove out of the parking lot, heading for the Anderson Freeway a few blocks away. They followed the steady pace of traffic westward towards LAX, then headed north on the San Diego freeway, before finally reaching the westbound Ventura freeway on their passage out of Los Angeles County.

Janice kept up a constant chatter about her work and friends, easily absorbing the time and miles. Within an hour they were well into Ventura County, passing through Camarillo. Clarene maintained a steady pace, as the old, but powerful El Dorado carried them forward in pleasant comfort on the lightly traveled, divided highway.

"Tell me about Victor," said Janice, inquisitively.

"We've been together a long time," said Clarene, "ever since I did a reading for him about ten years ago. We stayed in touch and when I opened the Institute, he came to the open house to congratulate me. We talked about the kinds of classes I wanted to offer and he suggested that I add one on past lives. I told him I would – as long as he taught it."

"Is that all he does? He seems to be there a lot."

"He's spending a lot of time there now, working on his book. He used to conduct past life sessions in his home for clients and made some money doing it."

"The inflection in your voice makes it sound like something happened."

"Yes, her name was Sheila. She was one of his clients, a very successful free-lance writer. Victor was infatuated with her youth – she was over twenty years younger than he was – and by her beauty and intellect. Surprisingly, she was attracted to him, too, probably as an authority figure, and the next thing they knew, they were married."

"Second marriage for both?"

"Actually it was the first for each of them. He had waited and waited for the right woman to come along, but all he found were older women who wanted their own way. When he found out Sheila was interested in him…well, neither one of them gave a lot of consideration to what they were doing. She had a flair for excitement and drama that he couldn't handle, and he became jealous and possessive.

"The more he tried to rein her in, the more she acted to prove he couldn't. In the end, she ran up some hellacious charges at Nordstrom and Bullocks on his American Express card, just to break his will. They had a very acrimonious divorce. She had a really good attorney and he's now paying off the bills, living in a studio apartment with what's left of his possessions."

"How sad for him. Is he all right?"

"Victor is bitter about Sheila and the legacy she left him. But, he's a survivor. He's very strong-willed and has no trouble knowing what he wants and finding a way to get it, either directly or indirectly. Once he pays off her debts, he'll soar again."

"You seem to get along well with him."

"Not always. You haven't seen us when we get going at each other."

"I'm sorry, I…I didn't mean to…"

"Don't get me wrong," Clarene quickly added, "Victor and I

are really the best of friends, we understand each other very well. He and I just see different sides of the same issues at times. The problem we have is that he is easily wounded by criticism, sometimes even the most constructive of comments can be taken by him as insults. And, you know me, I'm tough and independent, telling it like it is.

"I should be more considerate of his Cancer personality, but I'm not. He's a true Crab – at the slightest provocation or threat he retreats into his shell, waiting and hiding his ambitions until safer times are at hand. Sometimes, to protect his inner vulnerability, he will turn into the bully; out to get others before they get him.

"But," Clarene continued, "let me hasten to list his attributes: he is loyal, devoted to his past lives work, highly intuitive, friendly to his students, has a photographic memory and loves history."

"He looks European," said Janice. "Is he from the old country?"

"No. That's just the way he dresses. He grew up in Pasadena. His parents were both second generation Americans. I think his father was Polish and his mother was Hungarian. His real name is Wiktor Aleksanski, but it quickly became Victor Alexander when he started school. His father was in the Merchant Marine during the Second World War but never made it home. Victor claimed to have received psychic messages from him for years after."

"Messages? What did his father tell him?"

"To never give in when he was right. He taught him to rebel against authority and restrictions. In my opinion, that's what created most of the problems Victor faced when he grew up. His mother was, by nature, an overly demanding and domineering women. Her disposition only worsened when she had to become the father, too, for him and his two older brothers."

"Does he still see his brothers?"

"I don't think so. They picked on him a lot. He never met their expectations, nor his mother's. They both climbed the ladder of success in their professions – one's a lawyer, the other's a doctor, I think."

"Bill Edwards told me Victor was in the Navy, but didn't like being on a ship."

"The cold war was still going when Victor graduated from high school. At eighteen, he had to sign up for the draft. Since his father had gone to sea, he wanted to volunteer for the Navy, but his mother and brothers browbeat him into going to college, instead. So, he went to Pasadena City College for two years, *then* enlisted in the Navy. What a disaster that was! This is a guy who'd been taught to defy authority and he found himself living in the midst of the worst absolute authority he could imagine – shipboard life under a demanding Captain. He couldn't take it and fought to get out. Eventually, the Captain was glad to be rid of him and transferred him to a land base on the East Coast."

"How old is he? He looks close to sixty."

"Fifty-nine, last month."

"Is he writing a historical book? You said he was into history."

"He's very interested in history. It's a Cancerian trait. But, his book is on past lives regression. He'll get it done one of these days and then pay off the bills Sheila left him."

They were now a few miles east of San Ramon on the Coast Highway, paralleling the ocean. Clarene looked out her side window at the waves mildly curling towards the sandy beach. It was low tide. In the far distance, one of the Channel Islands forced its image through the haze.

"I've used his historical abilities at times. Just this week, for instance, he did some research for me relative to a couple of dreams I've had."

"Sounds intriguing. I read somewhere that some psychics have dreams predicting the future. Do you have dreams like that?"

"Yes, at times. They're called premonitions. In the last week I've had two on the same subject: about a dam that's going to be destroyed and the chaos and havoc the rampaging waters are going to cause. I was so disturbed, I went to Victor for help."

"Where is the dam?" Janice twisted in the seat to look directly at Clarene. "Are you going to try and stop it?" Janice was eager to be part of the action.

"I'm trying. I sure hope I can. That's one of the reasons for this trip."

Janice was momentarily taken back. "I thought we were going to confirm my past life regression."

"That's the other reason. They're both tied together."

"They are?" Janice was incredulous. "How?" It sounded like she *was* going to be part of the action!

"As I said, I went to Victor for help. The dream was so real, I knew it would happen, unless I stopped it. But I didn't know where the dam was, or why someone would want to destroy it. I knew if I could find out where it was, I could tell my friends in the Sheriff's department and they could do whatever they had to, to stop it. Or, if I could find out *who* was involved and *why*, that would be almost as good. The problem was, I didn't know any of that information and I was getting very upset about it. Victor was a big help, though. He said his psychic intuition told him there was a black-haired young woman and an old man involved."

Janice jerked her head toward Clarene, stunned at the words. "And the young woman was Antonia-Maria?"

"Yes," said Clarene, nodding. "Most importantly, he said the young woman would be coming to the Institute." She looked at Janice and smiled. "Of course, when you showed up with your blond hair, I didn't know you were the one, but I was drawn to you anyway. During the reading I did for you, when I saw you riding with your black hair flowing in the wind, I knew you must be Victor's dark-haired young woman. When I told him about you, he agreed. We were very pleased you came back for the classes."

"I'm not sure I understand all this," said Janice. "What do

I...I mean, what does Antonia-Maria have to do with your dreams?"

"That's what I hope to find out. When you were regressed as Antonia-Maria, you mentioned Los Robles and then the name Los Robles appeared in my second dream. The map shows a dam and a reservoir a few miles to the east of Los Robles, in the same general direction that Carlos took Antonia-Maria. It could be the one I'm looking for."

Janice beamed. She loved mysteries and here she was, in the middle of one. She couldn't help being excited and wondered what Teri would say if she knew what she had started.

"Will you tell me about the dreams?"

"Yes, but Antonia-Maria was not in either of them. The connection to her came from you and Victor." As they drove west along the coast from San Ramon, Clarene described her dreams, giving as many details to Janice as she thought she could handle.

The wide, four-lane highway continued to parallel the ocean for many miles before turning inland and climbing through the coast range of mountains. As they drove through a gently curved tunnel in the rocky foothills, Clarene had the ominous feeling of being followed, but upon clearing the tunnel, could find nothing in her rear view mirror to cause alarm.

"Are we getting close, now?" Janice asked restlessly, as they crested the top of the road and started down the long grade to the Los Robles Valley.

"It's not far," Clarene responded, eager herself to get the driving over. "A couple more miles and we'll turn right, then it's about four miles from there to Los Robles."

Janice looked out the car window at the low dry hills on either side of the road, densely covered with dried grass and weeds mixed with stunted chaparral, so typical to Southern California in July.

After they reached the exit and turned right onto the Los Robles Highway, the character of the land changed. In place of the dry hills, they were greeted with vast, open spaces of lush horse and cattle ranches, framed by the grayish-green mountains in the far distance. Everywhere they looked Oak and Sycamore trees dotted the stately fenced fields. All this in sharp contrast to the dry clay and rocks of the Rio Tranquilo riverbed traversing in the background, far to the right.

As they drove along the peaceful, pine bordered, two-lane thoroughfare leading to Los Robles, Clarene looked at her watch. "It's almost noon. There's a rest area up ahead," she said, pointing through the windshield. "We can stop there and eat the lunch you fixed."

"Sounds great," said Janice, anxious to get out and stretch. "I've been hoping we'd stop soon."

Clarene slowed the car for the turn-off to the rest area. The gravel crunched under the tires as they came to a halt just yards from one of its pre-cast concrete tables with attached benches.

Clarene opened the trunk and helped Janice remove the picnic basket. While Janice took it to the table, Clarene dawdled at the back of the car, scanning the road in either direction. Again she saw nothing to cause concern.

"Something wrong?" Janice called out. Even at a distance, she noticed the look on Clarene's face. "Are you picking up something about Antonia-Maria?"

"No. It's something else, one of those things we psychics have to live with."

"I don't understand."

"I keep picking up some sort of odd energy. It's strong enough for me to know it's there, but not strong enough to identify. It's beginning to bug me a little."

Shrugging her shoulders, she went to the car, opened the glove compartment and took out her map of the Los Robles Valley. Joining Janice, she spread it out at the end of the table and began to point out the various landmarks.

Los Robles and its tourist attractions, including the Mission Santa Delores, were clearly marked, as was the Los Vaqueros Dam and recreational area further to the east. As they looked at the various points of interest, Janice spotted the words "historical site" in tiny print, near the road by the dam.

"What's there, I wonder?" she asked, pointing to the spot.

"I don't know," answered Clarene. "We can stop if you want, when we drive that way."

Janice looked at the map for a few more moments. Tracing the main highway with her finger, she followed its path eastward through the valley, upward through the mountains and then down into San Ramon. She wondered what the road and scenery would have been like in Antonia-Maria's time. She also traced the other roads north from the Santa Delores Mission, trying to visualize Antonia-Maria's last few miles on the coach as she had approached the rest stop. Nothing clicked in her mind.

They ate quietly, each in their own worlds, not wishing to intrude on the other. When they'd finished, Clarene said, "This is *your* adventure, too. Is there anywhere you feel drawn to?"

"No," Janice replied. "I feel very comfortable being here. If it's all right, I'll just follow your lead and see what happens."

"That's fine," responded Clarene, as they got underway again. "Keep your eyes open for the historical marker. I'll stop, if you see it."

The road lead them through the picturesque village of Los Robles – no need to stop at the Mission Santa Delores, they both agreed – and finally past some magnificent horse ranches, before merging with the wide, two-lane Valley Highway. They easily joined a few other cars speeding eastward, following the curvature of the land. At the bottom of a long, gentle grade, the highway flattened out before crossing a bridge over the dry Rio Tranquilo riverbed.

Casually taking in the scenery as she sped along, Clarene was well into the middle of the narrow, concrete bridge before the SUV, its brakes locked and skidding to its fate, abruptly slammed itself across her vision. She shuddered, then tried to dispel the specter from her mind as she gripped the steering wheel, desperately holding the Cadillac on her side of the road.

Once over the bridge, she forced herself to breathe deeply and measuredly, gaining back full control of her mind and body.

"Is that the bridge?" Janice shouted the question, tensely. "Don't tell me that's the bridge."

"Yes. But, in my dream, the SUV was traveling in the other direction – I didn't recognize where I was, until its image swerved across my mind."

Clarene drove on in silence, regaining her composure as the low hillsides, now laden with scrub oak and dried, brownish grasses slipped past on her right. To her left, open vistas of clay and more dried grass were interspersed with random sections of fenced range, confining small herds of Angus and Hereford cattle.

As the miles passed, the highway narrowed…then widened, climbed…then dropped, twisting its way eastward through the encroaching foothills toward the dam and recreational area.

They were within a mile of the entrance when Janice cried out abruptly, pointing and wiggling her finger toward Clarene's side of the car.

"There it is! There it is!" she exclaimed. "The historical marker is over there, on the left!"

Flinching at the sudden outburst, Clarene applied the brakes and steered the car to the other side of the highway, bringing it to a stop on the shoulder near the sign. They both got out to read it.

A REST STOP FOR
TRAVELERS BETWEEN MISSION
SANTA DELORES AND MISSION SAN
RAMON WAS IN USE NEAR THIS
SITE FROM 1820 THROUGH 1829.
ONLY PORTIONS OF THE FOOTINGS
REMAIN OF THAT STRUCTURE, SINCE
ITS ADOBE WALLS WERE TAKEN AND
USED FOR THE STAGE COACH
OFFICE ERECTED IN
LOS ROBLES IN 1880.

Janice felt the hair at the back of her neck stand up as a shiver engulfed her body. She could see the building in her mind, its dark exterior silhouetted well off in the distance against the cloudless sky; smoke wisping from its chimney upwards through the surrounding trees. She stood motionless, deep in thought, retracing the images of the coach and the guards in her mind, trying to sort them out.

"The rest stop wasn't here," she said after a moment. "It's too open here, it had to be more to the north, out there, near that large grove of oak trees." She pointed to an area about three hundred yards away.

"Do you want to walk out there?" Clarene asked. "I'll go with you, if you want."

"No. It's not necessary. Carlos stopped us before we got there." She paused, contemplating that situation; "The guards would have done away with me if I hadn't escaped." She hesitated, as the scene at the coach continued rebuilding in her mind. After a moment, she quietly exclaimed, "And yet…I didn't really escape anything, did I?"

Clarene put an arm around Janice's shoulder and guided her back to the car. "Let's go up to the dam and see what's there."

As Clarene started to get back in the car, she whipped around to look back down the highway, catching a glimpse of a dark-colored vehicle parked off the road in the distance. She stared at the spot for a few moments, but it did move.

She sat down behind the wheel and adjusted the rear view mirror, watching intently. The odd energy she'd sensed before was back.

Less than a mile later, they had reached the entrance to the Los Vaqueros dam and recreational area. Clarene waited for two campers and a motor home to enter before driving forward to the entrance booth. She paid the day rate to the operator, took her receipt and descriptive brochure, then drove slowly down the asphalt roadway through a profusion of well-attended pine and oak trees toward the lake. Along the way she passed many RV's parked in their spaces.

At the end of the road, the broad vista of the dark blue lake burst into view. Its boat docks dominated the scene, stabbing like forks into the huge reservoir. Since it was a Friday, only a few slips were empty, waiting patiently for their occupants to return from an afternoon of sailing or water-skiing.

The low hills on the far shore were covered with dark green chaparral, studded with clumps of trees and shrubs, all enjoying the nearby water. Just above the edge of the lake, a wide band of white on the shoreline revealed the year's high water mark. In the background, the tall mountains thrust their rounded peaks skyward declaring their stature and prominence.

Clarene parked the El Dorado in the lot to the right of the docks. She and Janice waited for a moment, orienting themselves, before getting out to walk to the pebble-strewn beach not far from them.

"What a magnificent sight!" Clarene proclaimed. "And, what a huge lake. I can't see the ends of it," she said, looking in both directions. Then, turning her face to the breeze coming off the water, she added, "That air sure feels good on a hot day, doesn't it?"

Janice murmured her concurrence, but her mind was already exploring the landscape, trying to match it with images from her time as Antonia-Maria. Clarene watched her, letting the young woman go at her own pace as they walked along the shore, sometimes side by side, other times apart. She too, became engrossed in the surroundings, but for her own reasons.

Far down the beach from the docks, they came upon a bend in the lake and, as they walked on, the long, granite-faced, rear side of the dam began to reveal itself. Clarene thought it to be at least a quarter-mile across. Truly magnificent!

No boats were near it and she soon saw why: there was a sign on a small buoy floating in the water about a hundred yards uplake. It's bold lettering warned boaters to stay away from the dangers of the spillways at the dam's far-left side. As she walked on, the three massive gates came into view. A wide dark band across their upper edges confirmed the previous high water mark she had seen near the boat docks.

Clarene scrutinized the gates, comparing them to what she had seen in her first dream. They looked so massive, so mighty in their purpose – yet she knew they could easily be flung aside by the explosions she hoped to prevent. There was no doubt in her mind that this was the same dam and lake. No doubt whatsoever!

She wondered if she could get closer, but saw the path ended only a few yards from where she stood. She saw the roadway across the top of the dam was also inaccessible, for a chain link fence and gate blocked the entrance on the far end. No matter, she didn't need to go up there, anyway. Now that she knew this was the place, she could concentrate on 'who' and 'why' and not have to worry about 'where' anymore.

She mused on that for a moment. There were only three of them that knew about the gold and the map. Even if someone else had found out, what good would it do them, if the cave couldn't be located? It didn't make sense to blow up the dam, just to start looking around for a cave that collapsed in an earthquake almost 200 years ago. No, you'd have to know exactly where it was to start with! And if you knew that, why not just dive down to it?

At that moment Janice rejoined her, interrupting her thoughts.

"This is all so different from what I saw in the regression," she said, solemnly, "Back then, we were in an arroyo, a dried-up riverbed. It was wide, with small boulders and rocks everywhere, and lots of dead, scraggly looking weeds sticking out of the cracks in the ground. The foothills were dry and brown. Even the mountains looked grubby. But, look at it now, there's this huge lake and the hills are covered with trees and shrubbery. What a contrast! Even the chaparral looks healthy."

She stopped for a moment and gazed at the lake, before continuing. "The brochure we got at the entrance says there was an old road down there by the riverbed. Says it was built by the Spanish for travel between the Missions. It also says that it was later widened and paved as the main road through the valley until the dam was constructed and the lake covered it over."

She paused for a breath, then went on. "So, the old unpaved road the Spanish built, must be the one I was on when Carlos stopped the coach. Starting from where I think the rest stop was, I would say the area where the cave was, or is, must be up there by the docks." Her tone of voice was firm, positive. Clarene moved closer, not wanting to miss a word.

Sweeping her hand across the vista, Janice went on, "The hills look similar to when Carlos and I rode through here...except..." The firmness in her voice trailed off, hesitation showing through, "... except they don't seem to be as high. I guess it's because I was down in the riverbed then, and now the viewpoint is different."

"Things change over time, Janice," Clarene counseled. "What happened to Antonia-Maria took place almost two centuries ago. Wind and rain have softened and altered the features, trees have died, and new ones have grown. It doesn't have to be exactly the same now, to be the same place."

Janice nodded and looked more closely at the hills. "I wonder if the cave is still there?"

"Probably not," Clarene fibbed, not wanting Janice to get concerned about Antonia-Maria's remains. She felt it best for now to let it be.

They began walking back toward the boat harbor, arm in arm, Janice deep in reverie while Clarene kept scanning the trees and hillocks on her side of the lake. The odd energy was back and becoming very strong.

A moment later, she sensed him, before actually seeing him in the trees up to her right. At first it looked as if he might have been dumping garbage in a trash container – but then she realized he'd actually been watching them! He disappeared as quickly as he had appeared, melding into the pine trees, out of sight.

She had not seen his face and his shape had been obscured in the foliage of the surrounding trees. Her mind clamored to know who the man was and why he was watching them? Frustrated, she mentally took herself to task. One of the drawbacks to being psychic, she knew, was that it was hard to work on a conscious level with things that directly affected her. She could work with the energy around other people and develop a sense about them, but when it came to those things that affected her, it didn't work well at all. She searched the trees again and not finding a trace of him, swore at herself. Damnit! Why not just go up there and track him down?

Clarene actually started to go, but quickly remembered Janice – walking alone now, absorbed in her past, oblivious to her surroundings. Exasperated, Clarene turned away from the hill and trotted the distance to catch up with Janice, taking her by the arm. They walked on together in silence, past the boat docks, past the parking lot, crunching water-stained pebbles underfoot each step of the way along the path.

Janice stopped and began staring at the far shore.

"What do you see?" Clarene asked.

"I see where the cave was!" she exclaimed, pointing to a spot at the water's edge. "See that huge, streaked, jagged boulder over there?"

Clarene nodded that she did.

"I remember seeing it just before the horse ran away. I was fascinated with its shape and size. It was high up on the hill above the entrance to the cave. It's the same boulder, I know it is!" Suddenly her hands shot up to cover her eyes, trying to hide the terror of the past as it came to life again.

Clarene grabbed her and put her arms around her. She held her tightly, knowing what was going through her mind, knowing it was best not to say anything.

Clarene waited for a few moments before offering a suggestion to break the hold of the moment. "Do you remember what I've been saying about releasing your past? Well, now's the time for you to start forgiving yourself, and Carlos too, for the things you both did to end up in that cave." She dabbed a tissue at Janice's face. "I'll help you, if you like. It may not come easily."

Janice nodded, but her mind was still in the cave. The afternoon sun glistened off the lake, highlighting a few speeding skiers knifing through the water, scattering the lake birds as they passed. "I wonder if anyone ever came looking for us?" she asked, wistfully.

Clarene did not answer, merely touching Janice on the elbow as she started back to the car. "Come-on," she said, "let's get your face back on."

As they walked to her Cadillac, Clarene's thoughts returned to the man in the trees. Maybe he hadn't been watching them, after all. If so, it was probably just as well she hadn't gotten to him, for she would have made an ass of herself. On the other hand, if had been watching them, then chasing him would have tipped her hand that she knew. Either way, she was better off.

* * *

It had been a long day for him and he was tired. First had been the quick trip to San Ramon in the morning and then after returning to his Los Robles ranch, he had decided to come to his favorite haunt and ruminate on his favorite subject: the destruction of the damn dam. He quietly stuffed his binoculars into the large backpack on the ground beside him and got up, stealthily picking his way back to his vehicle.

He turned around often, keeping an eye out for them as he walked. He was sure he had seen their car in front of him on the way to Los Robles. And now, there they were again, their presence this time keeping him from reaching the rear of the dam. He hadn't seen them before, didn't know who they were and certainly didn't want to have them see him! When he saw the

Cadillac leave the parking lot and turn onto the paved roadway, he knew he could not keep walking towards his own vehicle without being seen. Changing direction, he began walking closer to the RV's, keeping them between him and the road.

* * *

Clarene noticed the green vehicle as they drove up the hill past the daytime picnic area. "That looks like Bill Edwards' Blazer, over there," she said to Janice, pointing out the window.

"Bill Edwards' Blazer? Where?" Janice suddenly perked up.

"Back there in the parking lot. But there's a million dark green Blazers in the world. I don't know why I thought it was his."

"Where?" Janice persisted. If Bill was around, she wanted to know it.

"Over there, parked next to one of the picnic tables on the right."

"Did you see him?" Janice was full of hope.

"No." Clarene was getting exasperated with the questions.

"Do you want me to go look?" Janice was still eager. "I could check to see if it really is his truck."

"No. That's not necessary." Clarene couldn't conceive of her Sheriff friend being here. It just didn't fit. He worked during the week and he would have no reason to be here. "It's after two, Janice," she blurted out to change the subject. "If we start back now, we may be able to avoid some of the Friday afternoon rush around L.A."

She showed her pass as they exited, turned right onto the Valley Highway and accelerated rapidly away from the congestion at the entrance. A minute later they passed the Historical Marker.

"It's been quite a day for me," said Janice. "It was kinda

hard there at the lake for a bit, but I really appreciate your bringing me along. Did you find anything that would help you to stop the dam from being blown up?"

"I know for sure it's the dam I saw in my dream. It's also easy to surmise that the reason someone wants to destroy it, is to get at the gold and the map. But there are only three of us that know about that, as far as I know. And, that doesn't account for the old man Victor said was involved. And, how would he know about the gold and the map being here? It doesn't make sense."

"Let me ask you this," Janice said, "how can you stop it if you don't know who's going to do it?"

"I don't know yet. But, I'm going to alert Bill Edwards when I get back to Bellflower; tell him what I know and ask for his guidance on what to do next. He'll help me."

"But, the dam's up here. There's not much Bill can do in this county, he's with the Los Angeles County Sheriff's Department."

Clarene hadn't considered that aspect. "Well, he'll just have to get in touch with the right people up here, then."

"I may not be too smart on these things, Clarene," Janice went on, carefully, "But don't you think Bill's going to have some problems trying to convince the Sheriff up here, that something's going to happen to their dam based only on the premonition of a psychic? I don't mean to offend you, but…"

Clarene looked at her for a few moments then nodded her head dejectedly. She lived in the real world, too. "You're right, of course. I keep trying to do this the easy way, always wanting instant answers and instant action. Fact is, I need a lot more information and that's going to take more time. Problem is, I don't think I have that much time!"

They drove on, past the bridge, past Los Robles and were soon back on the main highway leading to San Ramon and Los Angeles. As they started up the long grade away from the valley, Janice asked, "Did any of Victor's research have anything to do with Antonia-Maria herself?"

"Yes." Clarene reached over and patted Janice's hand. "He found an article in a California historical magazine. Let me tell you, it's a very intriguing story…"

TEN

Friday Afternoon

Carl McCormick had lived in the Los Robles Valley for his entire life. The McCormick name was synonymous with ranching. At one time it had also been synonymous with the Los Robles Valley Railroad and the stage line. The family had lived a relatively quiet life up to 1954 when San Ramon dammed up the Rio Tranquilo to create a reservoir to meet its water needs.

Carl had watched with disgust as the dam was completed and railed against it as "a symbol of unrestrained progress against the ranchers – for the benefit of those bastards in San Ramon!" On the day it was dedicated, the gates were closed and the springtime flow of water downstream was cut off forever. Carl thoroughly resented San Ramon's ability to exploit the rural, simple character of the land and its people, for their own purposes.

Two years later, with the lake almost filled, the throngs had started coming to the recreational area, clogging the valley with their traffic. Worse, many came back to stay, buying homes and driving up prices in the idyllic setting. They also brought their kids, quickly overloading the small, friendly school system. Their second cars and pickups soon wore down the unpaved side roads into dusty, pot-holed, car rattlers.

It was more than Carl could bear. Still, as a McCormick, he maintained his respectability, keeping his opinions to himself around strangers and low-keyed among his friends. Over the years, on those days when his hate for the dam got the best of him, he would go to the recreational area, hurling his thoughts at the back of the dam in vain attempts to destroy it and restore life as it was.

Earlier this Friday afternoon he had embarked on the same mission, but his plans had gone astray.

He had parked his old, brown Chevy pickup in the daytime picnic area, a few spaces away from the only other vehicle around, a green Blazer. At six foot three, he cut a stately figure in his rancher's jeans and boots. His gray hair and white mustache accentuated his angular face and broad nose.

He had started for the back of the dam, but the presence of the two women had forced him to walk towards the dock, instead, to avoid being seen by them on the path.

A few moments later, with the dock in view, he saw two men in animated conversation at the boat rental office. One was an older man and the other seemed to be the salesclerk. As Carl watched, the squabble continued, turning physical as the man grabbed the clerk by the arm and forced him to the side of the building, where he pointed to the far shore.

Whatever the clerk told the man, it was obvious to Carl that it had not pleased him, for he turned on his heel, and with a look of disgust on his face, tramped back up the hill to the Blazer in the parking lot.

Curious, Carl caned his way to the dock and approached the rental office. Seeing the youth inside, he walked up to the sales window and peered in, cane ready to tap for attention. But the boy looked up and immediately walked over to the window.

"Would you like to rent a boat, sir?" he asked pleasantly.

"Maybe," replied Carl in his deep voice. "I'm supposed to go out with a friend of mine. Was a guy just here?"

"Yeah. Wanted to know about scuba diving in the lake. Is that the guy you mean?"

"That's the one," Carl answered, leading the youth on. "Did you tell him he could?"

"No sir, of course not. It's against the rules. They allow boating, but no diving or fishing. Water skiing is allowed, but limited to certain areas."

"He's a nut at times. Where did he want to dive, this time?"

"On the far side." The boy opened the door and pointed to the hill on the far side of the lake. "Over there, by that big rock sticking out of the ground. See it?"

"Yes. I never know what he's going to do next. Did he say why he wanted to dive in that particular spot?"

"Asked me if I knew about a cave over there. I told him I didn't. All I know is that it's very deep with lots of old trees and branches. The fishermen used to love that area before they cut out fishing in the lake. But, I don't know anything about caves."

"I take it he wasn't too happy with your answer, eh?"

"Guess not, sir. He kinda stomped off." The youth walked back inside the office. "So, do you want to rent a boat?"

"Not right now. I'll see if I can catch up with him, first. Thanks for your help."

Carl leaned on his cane, looking at the huge rock on the far shore, wondering how the man knew there was a cave there and what he wanted with it. Scrutinizing the rock more closely, Carl marveled at its strange shape and coloring. He knew there had been geologists in the area in years past and wondered in the color indicated some sort of mineral deposit buried underneath. He looked at the boats on the lake for a moment, then turned and walked off the dock towards the picnic area and his truck.

ELEVEN

Friday Night

Clarene was tired. It had been a long day, full of strain as she faced the reality of her dreams. She'd come directly home after dropping Janice off at the Institute.

She didn't feel like having any dinner. Instead, she poured a glass of iced tea from the bottle in the refrigerator, then sat down in the living room to relax. The light of the early summer evening filled the room, giving it a comfortable glow. Her mind skipped through the images of the day: the pleasant ride up, the historical marker, the dam, the lake; she soon dozed off...then descended into a deep sleep.

In scant moments the lake returned, began to churn, then turn violent, as the cascading water thrust itself back into her mind, starting where it had left off at the bridge.

The rushing water heaved the jagged edges of the severed roadway high into the air and then recaptured them as the monster crashed and thundered its way through the next curve of the riverbed.

Los Robles was now only ten miles and a mere twenty minutes away.

Aptly named, Los Robles was carved at the turn of the century into the midst of an extensive grove of spreading oaks. With the advent of the dam, it had grown with the rest of the valley, and was now a tourist town that came alive on the weekends – its new-world Spanish atmosphere drawing thousands of visitors to shop in its specialty stores and eat its Mexican-styled foods. Its business district lay in a five-block area bounded by the Rio Tranquilo riverbed on the south and the Los Robles Highway on the north. A few homes from the early days still survived near the riverbed, but the majority were now in the low hills to the north of downtown. The eastern edge of town was defined by a road aptly named *Camino Nuevo,* running perpendicular from the Los Robles Highway past the Mission toward the riverbed. It crossed over the Rio Tranquilo on a low, wide two-lane concrete bridge leading to the cattle ranches beyond.

Less than eight miles away now, the rock-laden torrent surged forward over its ancient course, carrying its toll of debris toward its ocean destination. Onward it hurtled, swiftly closing the distance to Los Robles.

Most of Los Robles slept, but in the gathering light of dawn, the lights still burned in the loft of "The Golden Donkey," where five men continued their play in an all-night game of low-stakes poker. Two blocks away, the men of Engine Company One cleaned their equipment after having put out a suspicious fire in a dumpster behind the bakery. Directly across the street from the fire station, three women walked quickly on their way to that same bakery, to make ready for their usual early morning customers. While the full rays of the sun would be blocked from them by the nearby mountains for another hour, it was still light enough for them to see their way.

As the three turned right at the end of the block, five dogs and two cats trotted quickly past them in unison, hurrying away from the riverbed. The women each wondered at the unusual spectacle, but kept their thoughts to themselves.

The roiling torrent was now six miles away, gathering speed

and constantly shifting the undulating mass of rubble it was accumulating.

One other person was about, as well. He skulked near the center of town, stealthily heading for the water tower. His plan was simple: to empty it; since the Fire Department wouldn't hire him, they'd have to get along without him AND their water!

The three women reached the door of the bakery. Once inside, they set about their work, turning on ovens and moving ingredients from the refrigerators and storage shelves to the spotlessly clean worktables. Hairnets in place, they collectively eyed the work area, found it satisfactory and plunged into making doughnuts and pastries.

In the center of town, the water tower loomed in the gray vestiges of early morning as the young man crouched at its neatly trimmed, grass covered base. He knew his quarry well, for he had walked by it many times and he knew exactly what he wanted to do.

The tower was constructed of heavy gauge, green metal struts formed into a lattice upon which a huge, wide tank rested, some fifty feet above. The tank itself was painted black with three-foot high white letters on its side proclaiming Los Robles to all who cared to look. The steps leading to the tank had been removed years earlier to deny access to the graffiti artists. No one ever imagined someone would deliberately set out to destroy it.

The young man started climbing the outside of the lattice, strut by strut. Around his neck and shoulders he carried seventy feet of tough, three-quarter inch rope, a loop already formed at one end. He knew from his inspection a few nights earlier that the lever of the emergency drain valve at the bottom of the tank was rusted and impossible to open by hand. In his juvenile mind he needed only to attach the rope, climb down and then holding onto it tightly, jump the last few feet to jerk the valve open.

His steady climb was impressive, but no one saw it. His plan of execution was stupid, however, for not only was the lever rusted in place, it was also locked with a half-inch thick metal pin to prevent accidental release of the water. Misjudging the dawn, he found himself hurried and was oblivious to the metal pin as he attached the rope. He tugged to test its hold, then dropped the other end and climbed down.

Nearing the bottom of the tower, he grabbed the rope, pulled it taut, then looked around to see if anyone was watching. Ignoring the strange noise in the distance and the possibility of the deluge that would drop on him if the valve opened, he jumped.

In the next block, the firemen completed the clean up of their equipment and waited for the end of their shift. It was too late to go back to bed and too early to eat. Some snoozed, while others shaved. The muffled sounds of rushing water a scant four miles away were covered by the constant surging of filtered air from the ducts inside the station.

At the tank, the young man cursed the lever for failing to open and climbed back up the lattice work about five feet to try again. This time he wrapped the rope around his waist. Leaving a short length of the rope free, he jumped. The slack jerked taut instantly, slamming his stomach into his lungs, leaving him dangling in mid air, dazed and gasping.

But not for long. Angrily ignoring pain, logic and self-preservation, he grabbed the latticework and, once more, began to climb. When he reached a height of fifteen feet, he readied himself to jump again, but the growing crescendo coming from beyond the bridge stopped him. Overwhelmed with curiosity, he ignored the valve and climbed still higher to see what was making all the noise.

Only a mile from the bridge now, the torrent grew louder and began to widen into a bludgeon as the walls of the riverbed began to fade and flatten.

At the Golden Donkey, Jose Villalobos was restless – the cards had been unfriendly all night and he had been steadily losing, a little here, a little there. Nevertheless, he savored the outings, for none of the friends really cared whether they won or lost; only the game itself was important. They had been playing together for over ten years.

They usually started at nine and finished up promptly at eight the next morning, just in time to go to the bakery and grab some fresh doughnuts and free coffee.

They were all in their sixties and had met during the construction of the Los Vaqueros dam. Jose had stayed on when the dam was completed, opening the Golden Donkey as a small venture, selling imported Mexican pottery and art objects. He offered a wide variety of items that seemed to please his ever-growing clientele and expanded the size of the store often to match its popularity. The loft in which they played had been an early addition.

Jose looked at his cards and folded. He stretched in his chair, then got up and walked to one of the three large windows facing the river and opened it wide. He drew in a barrel-chested breath of fresh air, re-lit his cigar and was starting back to the table when he heeded the deep rumblings in the near distance. He stopped to listen intently.

The others at the felt-covered poker table, who had turned to enjoy the slight breeze coming through the open window, were startled at Jose's intent gaze and cocked ear. They all got up and went across the room to join him.

The churning mass was now less than a half mile from the bridge, its thunderous glut pushing rapidly across the old riverbed, a roaring signal to all that lay before it. As the morning light dismantled the shadows along its path, the maelstrom gathered momentum, rapidly closing with the bridge.

The steel gate, still in the forefront, slipped to the right as it passed over an indentation in the riverbed. As it did, its long, curved edge slammed into the boulder strewn bottom, caught for a moment, then tumbled free as the mighty current cast it forward side over side. Like an undulating monster, it quickly arched its back up and over, again and again as the gate was thrust ever closer to the bridge.

Abruptly, with one end high out of the water and the other at the bottom of its roll, the gate slammed flat against the concrete railings of the bridge with a jarring, thunderous smack!

Firmly held in place and shuddering end to end from the collision, the gate immediately blocked the mass of water behind it like a giant hand. Instantly, the accumulated rubble and debris that had been flowing freely were forced to the left, under the center section of the bridge. There, it quickly accumulated, filling the space between the shallow riverbed and the bottom of the bridge. As if planned, it slowed, then totally stopped the flow of water there, as well.

The torn and shattered oaks and sycamores that followed were skewed even further to the left where they too, became helplessly entangled under the bridge, shutting off the last channel for the natural flow of the torrent. Groaning as it smashed against the barriers, tons of water hurtled high over the obstacles, repeatedly trying to regain the riverbed on the far side.

Back on the right side of the bridge, the curved gate skewed a bit, suddenly forcing a gully-sized torrent up and over Camino Nuevo into Los Robles itself. Ever fed from behind, the torrent quickly careened towards, then through the town's business section. The small jewelry store at the corner of Camino Nuevo and Del Rio was demolished in seconds.

Watching from the window, Jose and the others stood paralyzed in uncomprehending terror as the unbelievable scene erupted before their eyes. They seemed frozen, unable to breath.

Inside the bakery, on the backside of the block with the jewelry store, the roar of the water was deafening to the three women. Seconds later, it crashed through the rear doors of the concrete-block building, smashing its way to the front where it destroyed the retail sales area, scooped up display cases, and scattered yesterday's pastries and two coffee urns, before exploding through the windows. In its wake, water swirled through the kitchen area, reaching out for the three women, who climbed terror-stricken onto the worktables. There they would remain, in shock, until rescued.

In the firehouse, an alarm went off, then a second and third as the water crashed through structure after structure, activating security systems. The firemen jumped to their trucks. With sirens wailing, they roared forth through the open doors of the station – directly into the path of the hurtling mass as it crossed over Avenida Chipultapec towards them.

In the next block, the young man in the water tower watched all of it in terror, then scurried further up the latticework, seeking dubious sanctuary. The rope, still attached to the release valve, tangled about his body as he climbed in desperation. He fought to free himself with one hand, while still pulling himself upward with the other.

The boundless water, still rushing and churning, headed down Avenida Chipultapec, straight for the tower. Realizing what could happen to him in his precarious perch, he forgot why he was there and leaped off the latticework; but the rope around his waist pulled taut and jerked him back into the steel cross pieces, knocking him unconscious, body dangling downward. An instant later a battering thrust of blackened water collapsed the latticework around him. Its release valve still intact, the tank fell and burst, adding its own contents to the maelstrom.

Jose and his friends in the Golden Donkey gathered their senses at last and scrambled through the door leading outside from the loft, then down the steps to the street level on the back side of the building. Together, they pushed and pulled each other as they ran to eventual safety. Jose watched in horror as The Golden Donkey was torn away from its foundations and swept downstream in broken sections by the torrent of devastation.

Block after block was inundated, smothered and crushed as the mass moved oppressively forward. The brick walls of the bank were smashed, its vault maimed, but left standing. Ten other stores and six restaurants also fell prey to the massive, aquatic attack.

City officials would later be amazed to find that only one home was damaged, none destroyed.

A long, frightening block from their station, the firemen and their trucks finally came to rest on higher ground. Alive, but soaked, they climbed out and watched in fascination as the torrent receded and moved west to rejoin the old riverbed.

Back at the bridge, the water continued to hammer at the trees and rocks under the far-left side trying to re-open a path. It soon created one, freeing up part of the constrained energy, which then attacked the rubble under the center section, clearing and shoving it downstream, too, out of the way.

With its flow almost fully re-established, the pressure of the water on the gate on the right side magnified, causing its curved bottom to break free. Once it was loose, it twisted sideways, then slammed across the nearest support column, shattering it on impact. The roadway above instantly dropped into the swirling mass and started moving westward.

Unable to support itself against the increased pressure, the center column collapsed too, abruptly dropping another section of the bridge into the torrent.

Moments later the violent, frothing mass finished clearing its way, gaining back its total freedom. With renewed energy and confidence, it surged forward, rapidly gathering back to its bosom the kin that had so viciously strayed through town.

Flowing aggressively now over the wide, old riverbed, it easily spread its muscular arms in a forceful, turbulent reach for the sea.

There were, of course, other bridges and other towns along the way.

TWELVE

Saturday Morning

Clarene was exhausted. The images of Los Robles being hammered by the roiling water in her latest dream had wakened her, then clamored through her mind the rest of the night, continuously merging with the violent images of the first two dreams. She had slept fitfully.

God, No more dreams! she screamed in her mind as the morning light finally rescued her. *I don't need anymore premonitions – I'm doing all I can! I've found the dam and I'm going to talk to Bill Edwards. So, no more dreams, please – they're tearing me to pieces!*

She sat up, dangling her legs over the edge of the bed, looking down at the tiny, yet visible veins around her ankles. This was no time to worry about them, though, and she quickly changed her focus to calling Victor, then stopped and looked at the bedside clock. What time was it? Would he be up? The green luminescent numbers held steady at 6:36 am. It had been twelve hours since she had come home, yet she couldn't remember what she'd done after that, or even getting undressed for bed.

In spite of the hour, she impulsively dialed Victor's number and waited, and waited, but the repeated ringing went unanswered. Replacing the phone in the cradle, she got up, slipped out of her nightgown and walked to the shower.

Two hours later she was in her office at the Institute, mildly curious as to why she didn't see Victor's car in the parking lot when she arrived, yet aware that it was Saturday, a time for personal errands and shopping.

She picked up the phone and pressed the automatic dialer to reach Bill Edward's office. She knew he sometimes worked Saturday mornings and hoped he would be in.

"Sheriff's Department, Edward's." The voice was pleasant, as she expected it to be.

"Hi there. This a voice from your future."

"And my past and present, too. How are you?" he said, leaning forward in his chair to be closer to the phone. His 5'11" solid frame easily filled the cheap metal and imitation leather chair provided by the Department. "Checking up on me?"

"Do I need to?"

"No. I just haven't seen much of you this past week. I hear stories around your place that you're up to your neck working with Victor on probing one of Janice's past lives. Something about a Mexican and buried treasure."

"Where did you hear that?"

"It seems to be common knowledge."

"My God! It never occurred to me that it would get out!" She paused, overwhelmed with the thought that her students were aware of the situation and one of them might exploit it, for personal gain. "How much do you know? How much have you heard?"

He told her. It seemed to be everything. Everything except the trip she and Janice had taken and her dream last night. He concluded his comments with an understated, yet affectionate, dig, "Must be very interesting to get that kind of attention from you," he added.

"I think you're about to find out," she replied, taking full advantage of the opportunity.

Alarmed at her frankness, he sat up in the chair, waiting for her to continue. But, when she didn't, he offered a hesitant response. "That sent a shiver up my back. You know, the kind you get when you know something's coming at you, but you don't know what it is, Or, how to protect yourself. What's going on, Clarene?"

"Bill, listen to me. You've known me for quite some time now, and I believe you trust me as a person, and as a psychic."

"Yes, I do." His statement was hesitant, though, seeming also to say 'so?'

"Hang-on," Clarene, went on, "I'm leading up to something. If you know about Antonio-Maria and the gold, then you have to know about the dam, as well."

"Yes."

"Well, it's not just a dream, it's a foregone reality, unless I can stop it! And you have to help me!"

"I'm willing to listen, Clarene. What do you have in mind?"

"I want you to help me stop the madman before he can pull it off, help me stop him from blowing up the dam! We haven't got much time, left!"

"How much time do we have? When's he going to do it? Who is the guy?"

"Oh Bill, that's the bad part, this is one of those cases where I simply don't know any of that – all I can tell you is that the pressure keeps building inside me with each new dream and I know it's only a matter of time now before it happens!"

"Each new dream? Have you had another?"

"Yes. Last night. This time the river took out another bridge and the town of Los Robles."

"Good God!"

"Bill, I want you to contact the Sheriff in Los Robles and give him warning. Will you do that? Will you do that for me?"

"Bluntly? NO. Where's your proof? What's the name of the person and when is he going to do it? Without that kind of information, no one is going to believe that story. We're going to have to have a substantial amount of proof to satisfy that rural Sheriff up there before anyone can contact him. Right now you don't know squat about who and when, and from what I've heard, you're not even certain as to why."

"That's true," she responded dejectedly, exhaling a deep sigh.

"You also only have assumptions as to where," Bill continued.

"That's also true. But, you know me, these dreams are real and so is the situation."

"Clarene, you live in a world that few people understand. Even those that deal with you know very little about how you really make it work. I live in a different world, a world of facts and just the facts. I've crossed over to your viewpoint on many occasions to satisfy the needs of law enforcement, but no matter where you've led us, we still have had to back it up with facts. We don't have any in this situation."

"Bill, I've led you a lot of places in our work together to solve homicides, and then you've dug up the facts from there. So, just take this as one more time that I'm leading you somewhere and work with me to get the facts!"

"I'd like to do that, Clarene, but I can't. When we use you, it's after the crime has occurred. There are circumstances and facts already in place. You come in when we need help following the leads provided by those circumstances and facts. What you're asking me to do is rely on a premonition, a situation not in existence and take action to prevent it. If there ever was a sure, slippery slope to career termination, this is it."

"So what am I supposed to do?" Her voice started to climb, desperate for his support. "If my friends in law enforcement won't take me seriously, what can I do? I still have to prevent it."

"I didn't say I didn't take you seriously! In fact, I believe you. But, you're going to have rely on using your psychic powers, not police powers, for the time being."

"Mr. Edwards, I don't have time!" Clarene's anger spilled over, taking control of her ability to think and act rationally.

"Come-on Clarene, listen to yourself. That's someone different from the person I know, talking. Remembering back to some of your classes, I'd say that was an ego yelling at me. And, if that's true, we've got a bit more than a lack of facts to overcome."

She was stunned by his words. They hurt, deeply, and she couldn't respond.

"Clarene, no matter what you think, I am your friend and I know that within you is the ability to solve this matter before it happens. For some reason you've gotten your ego all wrapped up with jumping ahead to the end, when what you need to do, is step back, remember your own teachings and meditate on the path you should follow."

"I won't be able to meditate, I'll have another dream!"

"Damnit, Clarene! Listen to yourself! Your ego's in control. Dump the ego and regain your inner self! What do I have to do, come over there and hold your hand?"

"Would you?"

Startled, he could only laugh.

She laughed, back.

Then they both began giggling and couldn't stop.

He was there in fifteen minutes.

* * *

"Sorry about that on the phone," she said, offering him a seat in her office. "I think I *am* losing it over this thing with the dam."

"Hey, Clarene," Bill replied, reaching out to touch her hand, "we all get that way one time or another when the pressure starts to build. Your problem is that you think you have to remain in control all the time, to always be the leader, so others will follow."

"If I don't, how will they respect what I have to say and teach?"

"You worry too much about that. People are smart, they know

that what you're offering is good for them. It's just that they aren't always ready to accept it at the moment you're offering it. It doesn't mean they've rejected it, or you."

"My, my, you did learn a great deal from my classes."

"Yes, I did. So let me take my Sheriff's badge off for awhile and become your mirror. Let me return the favor, so to speak."

"OK, but it may seem strange to me."

"Only if you make it so. Here's the deal as I see it. You've had some dreams that were not only premonitions, but also really scary movies. The scary movie part was so dominant that it distracted you from the real message – that someone was going to blow up the gates of a dam and create a lot of havoc.

"Now, a lot of people have premonitions. The difference between you and them is that you have the energies and talents to do something about it. But, while your efforts have produced some information, they've produced even more frustration. So, the real solution is to sit back, turn off the pressure completely and let the answers come to the surface in their own sweet time."

"I don't think we have anymore time!" She started to get adamant, again.

"Damnit! There you go again! What do always teach here? You teach that the answers always, always, come when you are ready to accept them! And, NOT BEFORE! As a matter of fact, don't you say that the answers are really there already, it's just that we're blinded to them by our egos?"

Clarene nodded her head, listening.

"So, again, the solution seems simple to me. Go off someplace where the energy of this Institute, and this building, and your home, and your ego won't have any effect on the outcome, and meditate. Let the answers come to the surface – I'm sure they're trying! It's up to you to let them come out on their own terms."

Clarene leaned back on the couch, smiling at him, shaking her head in amazement at the lesson he had just taught her. The

"Lesson of the Mirror," she would say later, for he had forced her to see the message she had been teaching others for years.

"I think I'll take a ride down to Balboa," she said, "and sit on the beach for awhile and listen to the pounding of the waves. I've always liked it down there, the ocean has such a way of rejuvenating me."

She stood up and tenderly shook his hand. "I'll call you when I get back."

THIRTEEN

Saturday Afternoon

Clarene held the phone loosely in her right hand, close to, but not touching her ear.

"Bill? This is Clarene," she said quietly, when he answered. "I'm back from the beach and I'd like to talk, if you can spare the time."

"Sure. Something came up after I got back and I got stuck here. I'm working on it at the moment, but if you can wait about an hour, I'll be over then." His voice was upbeat, hopeful for her.

"I'll be waiting, meet me in my office."

"Did you find what you were looking for?"

"Enough."

"Good for you!" he said, exuberantly. Now, maybe they could do something!

She hung up and left the white couch where she had been sitting, and walked down the hall towards the library, hoping that Victor had finally come in. He wasn't there and his car still wasn't in the parking lot. She started to get upset, but the relaxation of her time on the beach overrode the inclination and instead, she strode over to the social area for a cup of tea.

It was strangely quiet around the Institute, she thought. Where is everyone? A moment later, she realized she really didn't want anyone around now, anyway. Especially after her meditation on the beach. She now had answers; answers which must be shared with Bill Edwards before a plan of action could be devised. She had just picked up her tea and was starting back to her office, when four women came in through the outside door.

"Is this where the Psychic Fair is?" one asked. The others looked around, seeking the food and the tables of psychic readers they had expected.

"That was last Saturday," Clarene replied. "The next one will be in another three weeks. Come back then, we'd love to have you."

"Are you Clarene?" the same one asked.

"Yes. I run the Institute."

"Will you do a reading for us? We hear you're really good."

"I'd love to. I have some openings next week."

"Aw, can't you do it now?"

"I'm sorry, I wish I could, but I have a meeting scheduled to start in just a bit and it's important that I keep the appointment."

The women tried to convince Clarene to change her mind, but she remained firm. The meeting with Bill was just too important, and these women were only looking for predictions on when they could expect new lovers in their lonely lives. Clarene knew there weren't any prospects on any of their horizons and that would take a long time to gently get across.

As the four were finally leaving, Bill Edwards came up to the entry, let them pass, and walked in with a smile on his face. With his closely cropped dark hair, muscular build and thin mustache, no one would mistake him for anything but a cop.

"So it worked, huh?" he said.

"Yes, to a certain degree." Clarene replied. "Come up to the office where we can have some privacy and I'll fill you in."

A few moments later they were seated in the office, she on the white couch and he in a comfortable chair facing her.

"I still don't know when, but I do know that the old man that

Victor mentioned is very much involved. In fact, in my meditation, I saw him as a principle player, who has long thought of destroying the dam because of its intrusion into his and his family's lives. There was lots of symbolism about all of that. Sorting it out was relatively easy, once I let my ego get out of the way."

"Did you get a name?"

"I kept seeing the name 'Carl', and a steam engine and a bagpipe. I also saw him as a tall man, dressed like a rancher. He's older, but still active and probably has a mustache." She hesitated before sharing the next bit of information, but then decided he should know about it. "There's one more thing about him that kept coming up in my mind."

"What's that?"

"There's a tie between him and the man I saw in my second dream, driving the SUV that got caught on the first bridge the river destroyed. He was on his way to his Uncle's ranch in Los Robles."

"Isn't Los Robles near the place where Janice was attacked?"

"Yes, in her past life as Antonia-Maria. We went up there yesterday to look at the dam and see what we could learn."

"I'd heard that you'd found out where the dam was, but I didn't know you'd gone there. Find anything worthwhile?"

"I confirmed that it *was* the dam in my dreams. It matched perfectly. Janice also looked around up there and thinks she knows where the cave is. But the really interesting part is that I think we were followed."

"Followed?" His dark eyebrows arched up, the Deputy Sheriff in him fully alert.

"Yes. At first I was confused about that. I thought there were only three of us that knew about Antonia-Maria, and I couldn't figure out who would be following us, particularly if no one else knew."

"But, there *were* others, Clarene, it was all over the Institute."

"Yes. I can tell you I was very surprised when you told me

that. Obviously, Victor was the source, puffing up his ego and telling everyone how successful he had been in yet another past life regression; how he had helped Janice overcome her fear of men! I don't know why I was blinded to that aspect. Of course he would do it! He couldn't help himself."

"Well, not only that, Clarene. The students in the Tuesday night class couldn't help but see how she was when you had her join them that evening. She was distraught, red-eyed and could hardly hold herself together. Everybody wondered what was going on and they soon found out about the regression she had just experienced."

"Well, my friend," she said, emphasizing the point with her finger pointed at his chest, "I think someone in this Institute is going after the gold and the map. It came to me in my meditation, but for the life of me, I can't get a better handle on who. Which brings me to a big question I have for you. I saw a green Blazer like yours up at the lake yesterday, was it yours?"

"I wasn't at your lake yesterday, or any other day," he answered firmly, somewhat offended. "In fact, I didn't even have my Blazer around to use."

"You didn't?"

"No. Victor borrowed it to move some things. Said his Volvo couldn't handle the size of the boxes. I didn't see a problem, so I let him have it."

"Victor borrowed your Blazer?"

"Come-on, Clarene, what's your concern?"

"Don't you see? Someone from the Institute is involved with this thing about the dam, and then Victor borrows your Blazer, and then your Blazer shows up at the dam after I have a feeling someone is following us."

"If this gets anymore complicated, Clarene, you won't be able to say all that with just one breath."

"Why are you mocking me?"

"Remember, I'm a Deputy Sheriff. I think like a Deputy Sheriff. Let's not jump to conclusions. First, I've seen more than one green Blazer like mine in our parking lot. It's a popular model and color. I don't know who they belong to, and they're not here everytime I'm here. But, they do exist and I've seen them.

"Second, what purpose would Victor have in trying to get the gold and the map? You know, we have to look at motive and opportunity."

Clarene found herself on the horns of a dilemma. She didn't know what Bill knew about Victor's financial status and didn't want to go blurting it out. Worse, she felt bad about the things she had just implied about Victor. He hadn't shown up as a culprit in her meditation, so why was she suddenly being so hard on him? Was it because he had been reticent at the start to get fully involved with her in solving the matter? Was that it? Was she feeling petulant because her long time friend had not leaped immediately into the fray with her, even though he said he was committed, now? Good God, was her ego getting in the way, again?

"I don't know," she answered deviously. "Perhaps you're right. Who else, then? Who at the Institute stands to gain from this?"

"Well, I'm not going to interrogate them all, if that's what you have in mind."

"Of course not!" She started tapping her fingers on one of the cushions of the couch. "If Victor were here, I'd ask him directly and that would clear the matter up. But, he's not, and I don't know where he is!" She was starting to get truly frustrated again.

Bill looked at her intently, eyebrows raised in firm determination that said 'calm down'. It was enough. "Have you tried his home?" he asked.

"Yes, early this morning. There was no answer. I expected to find him here, but he hasn't shown up, yet. I just naturally started assuming the worst."

"All right, back to basics, then. If he's going to show up, he will, when it's the right time."

"What's the right time?" The voice in the doorway startled them both. It was Victor.

"Where have you been?" Clarene demanded. "I've been looking for you all day!"

"Why? Did you have another dream?"

"Yes! And, that damn water gets more vicious every time."

"You mean, your mental images of the water and the destruction it's going to cause are getting more vivid. The way you talk, the water has taken on a mind of its own." Victor removed his bifocals and cleaned them with his tie as he spoke, then put them back on.

"Yes, it's like it has," Clarene responded, ready to defend herself, if necessary. "I know that sounds absurd, but my mind has certainly fleshed it out." She stopped abruptly, stared at the Past Lives Teacher and again demanded, "Where have you been all day?"

"Driving back from Los Robles."

"Whattt??" What were you doing in Los Robles? Were you following me?"

"Yes, in a way. And, no, not really."

"That's double-talk, Victor, and you know it!"

"Well, I wouldn't have even mentioned it, except I found out something while I was there, something you need to know."

Clarene and Bill looked at each other. "Go on," they said, almost together.

"There was a man there. An older man, kind of distinguished looking, with a white mustache, driving a brown pickup truck."

"Why did you go there in the first place?"

"Because of you, of course. You demanded, *demanded, mind you*, that I get involved with this crusade of yours. So I did. And then you have the audacity – after I do a lot of work in the identifying the characters involved, and leading Janice to Antonia-Maria and Los Robles, and you to the dam – to dismiss me with a flourish of your hand, saying it was a girl thing and you and Janice would go alone! Well, damnit, Clarene, that's not the way it works!"

Clarene was stunned for the second time in days on the effect her actions and words were having on Victor.

"Victor. I didn't mean to cut you out. I was trying to protect Janice, woman to woman. I felt it was important. That's why I went alone with her."

"Clarene, as I've said before, for all your knowledge of people and your ability to read their minds and emotions, your don't know crap about men. I've decided to stand up for me in this situation. You may think you're going to get all the glory when this thing is solved and the Institute will take off with flying colors, but I've had a big hand in it, too! And, I'm certainly going to take my share of the credit and use it to promote my book. So, don't try to stop me!" He emphasized his words by removing his bifocals and staring at her with his determined hazel-green eyes.

"No one is trying to stop you, Victor! Quit acting like a little boy. I agree that you've made substantial contributions to solving this matter, but it's not over yet and there's a lot more to be done."

"Well, let me make it easier for you, then. The guy I told you about, had apparently seen me down at the boat dock and then came up to me later in the parking lot."

"I didn't see your Volvo there. What were you driving?"

"Bill's Blazer, of course. I think you already know that."

"Why did you take his Blazer?"

"I didn't want you to see me and I knew you'd recognize the Volvo, so I tried to borrow another car. When Bill heard me asking if anyone would consider lending me theirs, he came over and offered his Blazer. It would have been difficult to refuse under the circumstances and I gave him a lame excuse as to why I needed it."

"So were you behind us all the time?"

"Not really. It's not like I was spying on you. I was really interested in seeing the scene of the crime, so to speak, so I could take a measure of its energy. I needed that information so I could sort through the results and continue to contribute to solving the crisis. I mean that, I'm a part of this, and I'm going to help solve it!"

Clarene exhaled audibly and rubbed her forehead. "All right, all right. Of course you're a part of this! And so is Bill, now." She looked at the ceiling for a moment and then back at the two men. "Good God, am I ever getting lessons from the two of you!"

Suddenly a question flashed into her mind. "So what did you do with the tapes?"

"Tapes?" Victor asked.

"Yes, the tapes of the sessions with Janice. Where are they? Why are they gone?"

"I have them. They're not gone. I wanted to listen to them to get as much information as I could for my trip up there. I played them on the way up."

"Are they back here, now? I'm not getting on your case, since they're your tapes to start with, but Janice wants to hear them; even get a copy if she can."

"They're here and I'll be happy to make her a copy. Of course I will."

"So," she continued as if the subject of the tapes had never come up, "did this guy you met drive a train or carry a bagpipe?"

"That's good Clarene," Victor replied, nonplused by the quick change in subject. "A strange question, but good. You must be picking up something from my thoughts. Yes, his father owned the little railroad that ran through the valley. And, his Grandfather helped settle the valley. The valley means everything to his family. He spends a lot of time thinking about the old days when he was growing up there."

"Did he mention the dam? I'll bet he isn't happy about it being there and changing his valley around. Does he hate it enough to blow it up?"

"My god, Clarene! He's in his seventies. People in their seventies think a lot about the way things were in the past. That's probably because they can't do a lot of planning anymore about things in the future."

"So, is he the old, gray-haired guy you envisioned last week?"

"I don't think so. I thought about that when I first saw him, because he was old and gray-haired, but I felt no confirmation when I was talking to him."

"Did you get any feelings or sense anything?" Clarene wasn't happy with his answer.

"Why are you concentrating on this guy?"

"Because my meditation led me directly to him as the culprit. And, you've confirmed almost everything I sensed about him, except telling me he's the one!"

"Well, I don't feel that he is."

"Maybe that's because your mind was elsewhere. What had you been thinking about before he showed up?"

"I was thinking about the cave. I was wondering how to get to it."

"Why? Are you after the gold to pay off Sheila's debts?"

"God no! I'm trying to figure out how to get evidence to support the reality of Past Lives regression. If I could get to the cave and find something that clearly belonged to Antonia-Maria or Carlos, think what that would mean as proof to a skeptical public. That's what I want; that's what I need."

"This is about your book, then?"

"Of course, but it's also about getting closure for Janice."

"Did you get his name?" Clarene wanted to get back on track.

"Yeah, I think it was McCorkle or McCormick, something like that. First name is Carl." Victor laughed. "Bagpipes indeed, Clarene, bagpipes indeed."

"What did you talk about?"

"Said he'd seen me down by the lake. Told me he came there quite often and hadn't seen me before. Was curious who I was and wanted to meet me."

"Seems to be a direct kind of guy," Bill exclaimed. "The kind that is used to being in control, making things happen. The kind that can be very dangerous."

Victor stared at him in return, wondering why the comment was important.

"So where did he steer the conversation? What did you talk about?" asked Clarene.

"Calm down, Clarene. He's a very interesting kind of guy. We chatted about a lot of things. He has a large ranch near Los Robles and we talked about raising cattle. Told me a lot of other things, like that in the old days, when the road ran up the center of the valley, you could see caves in the side of the hills. Told me he thought the Indians used to hide in them after escaping from the Mission Padres. Now you can't see them anymore since the lake has covered it all up. We kidded about the fact that the only way to see those caves today would be to lower the water level."

Clarene waited for him to finish.

"I noticed he carried a cane," Victor continued, "and when he saw me looking at it, he told me that it was just for show. He liked the respect it got for him from younger people, but he didn't really need it."

"Interesting. I wonder what other deceptions he's good at." Clarene's brown eyes narrowed at the thought.

Victor ignored her and went on about his conversation with Carl. "Told me he was having problems with a small creek on his property that was dammed up by a deeply rooted tree stump and wondered if I had any suggestions as to how to clear it out. We talked about the use of explosives, but he didn't seem to know much about them, except that he knew his ranch hands kept some dynamite around for when they needed it. I told him that probably wouldn't work with his problem, though, since the stump was buried pretty deep and he couldn't light the fuse underwater. We finally figured out together that if he encased the dynamite in something to keep the fuse from getting wet, it might work. He invited me over to his place the next time I came up and then he left."

Victor's casual attitude alarmed Clarene. "You told him to encase the dynamite in something to keep the fuse from getting wet?"

"Sure, that's the way to do it. I don't know how he could accomplish that, but that's the way to do it."

"Do you have any idea what you have done?"

"No. What did I do?"

"Do you remember telling me in the library last week that the way to blow up the gates of the dam would be to use steel drums loaded with dynamite so the energy would be concentrated at the columns? Do you remember that?"

"He's trying to handle a little stump in a shallow little creek. This guy doesn't know about dynamite and he doesn't know about steel drums!"

"He does now, Victor," Bill stated quietly. "You told him."

"He's not going to blow the dam up!"

"Wanna bet?" Clarene and Bill said it in unison.

"Look, Victor," Bill went on, "in my business, we've run into a lot of really sharp con men. I mean, people who can smooth-talk their way into another person's confidence without ever raising a single blip on the radar screen of concern. These people are so totally adept at lying, that what they say isn't a lie anymore. Now, I'm not saying this guy, Carl, is a con man, but I do think he's very good at saying what he has to say to get what he wants. Think about it; how many people in today's world do you know that would walk up to a total stranger and engage him a conversation like you had? He paid a lot of attention to you, led the conversation where he wanted and when it got interesting, got information out of you that he needed, without a raising an eyebrow on your part."

Victor didn't say a word. He found a chair and slumped down, his round, stubby frame leaning precariously at the edge. Shaking his head from side to side in denial, he could only utter, "I can't be that gullible, I'm a psychic, for god's sake. Things like this don't happen to me!" The puffy pads under his eyes began to grow and protrude.

"Well it did!" Clarene said, angrily. "It can't be taken back, now that it's done. The only thing to do is get back up there and stop him before he does anything serious. In fact, let's take *full* advantage of what happened. We'll go to Los Robles and track him down. Then we'll go to the Sheriff up there with the facts and let him deal with Mr. McCormick or McCorkle, or whatever his name is."

"I'll look up the Sheriff's name for you," Bill offered. "Gather as many facts as you can and present them to him in a logical form and see where it goes. Remember, though, this is a psychic-based operation, not a police investigation. You can't use my name or say I'm working with you on this. That would back-fire on both of us!"

"All right," agreed Clarene. It's too late to start tonight, but we could leave at first light tomorrow. Victor, you drive, since this is your guy and we're going to *his* place. Janice and I will be your tourist passengers."

"The guy may be suspicious if I don't have the same car," he said, looking at Bill. "Maybe you could see your way clear to letting me use the Blazer again?"

"That's fine. I can't take a direct hand in this thing, but I'll be happy to help out this way. One thing, though, don't you think you ought to track down Janice and see if she's available? Tomorrow is Sunday and she may not be up to a long trip again, especially when she has to go to work on Monday."

"I'll call her now," Clarene said. "I want her to be part of this."

FOURTEEN

Sunday

Janice was early again, waiting for the others in the parking lot of the Institute as they arrived. Victor first, in Bill's Blazer, followed shortly afterwards by Clarene. She parked her Cadillac and walked briskly to join them.

The usual pleasantries out of the way, Victor soon had them speeding their way north to Los Robles. Clarene and Janice said little about his driving, for it was obvious he was determined to make up for his transgressions and get them to Los Robles in the shortest, safest time. This he accomplished in just over two hours.

Janice sighed relief as the town came into view. Victor heard it and commented that there was never any doubt they would arrive safely, without any speeding tickets.

"How can you be so sure about that?" Janice asked.

"Because I sent out the right energy clearing the road of hazards and cops."

"You can do that?"

"Sure," he said, showing off for the young woman, "so can you or anybody else. You just have to think positively and put out the right kind of positive energy."

"Right. Just put out positive energy. Like, I know how to do that."

"Have you ever had to get somewhere important and concentrated on getting through all the lights on green?"

"Yes."

"And, did you?"

"I was just lucky."

"Wrong. You were practicing basic personal energy management. Think what you could do if you let us teach you how to manage your entire life that way."

Before Janice could answer, Clarene interjected her own energy management. "We're here to find a guy named Carl. Let's get on with it!"

"How do we do that?" asked Janice. "Do you both use your psychic powers to see if you can sense him around here somewhere?"

"We use the phonebook."

"Oh."

Victor found a place to park in the business section. Clarene got out and strode over to the nearest phonebooth and began looking through the directory. She found nothing for a Carl McCorkle, but was successful with Carl McCormick. Jotting down the address, she headed back to the Blazer. The next stop was a local gas station to get a map of Los Robles, but they didn't carry any, so it was off to a drug store which didn't have any, either. Finally, they found one at a Real Estate sales office, but had to endure a hard sell about local opportunities and values before the map was released.

Enduring tiny print and two heads peering over her shoulders, Clarene finally found Carl's street on the map. Orienting herself to where they were, she showed Victor where they had to go. He started the Blazer and they were on their way.

Los Robles, itself, had an easy street layout to follow. But, once outside the main part of town, where the ranches spread out, the streets and roads were less formal, with signs that tended to be obscured by trees and shadows, making them far less visible. To add to their confusion, a road might suddenly dead-end and require backtracking to get to where they wanted by another route. It took time and was exasperating.

When they eventually reached the ranch, they found it to be an impressive spread surrounded by a four-foot high, white rail fence. Hundreds of cattle stood alone or in clusters on the vast, lush green carpet of grass that surrounded the main house and outlying structures.

At the main entrance, they found the wide wooden gate open and continued up the equally wide asphalt road to the main house. Along the way they passed a number of large sheds and storage buildings. A narrow creek meandered nearby but seemed empty of water.

The road was lined with Eucalyptus trees on either side, filtering their view of the surroundings, but the main house soon loomed into full view as the road curved to the left. It looked Victorian in age, but tastefully modern in color and upkeep. The old, brown pickup truck, parked near the front of the house, was not in keeping with the elegance of the home.

The front screen door opened as the Blazer came to a stop. Carl, himself, slowly walked to the edge of the porch, peering to see who was in the vehicle with Victor. Clarene saw that he was an imposing figure. Dressed in his usual rancher jeans and boots, his tall, stately frame was accented by well-groomed gray hair.

"Good morning," he called out to Victor in his deep voice. "This is a surprise."

"Good morning to you, too," Victor called back through the open window of the Blazer. "I'm sorry to intrude, but you did say to come by and I have some friends that wanted to meet you. Is it OK?"

"It's fine. Come on in. Have some coffee."

"Thanks, we will."

The three got of the Blazer and walked up the steps to the porch. Victor introduced the women to Carl, who scrutinized the two before ushering them all into the house.

Janice was overwhelmed with the stately beauty of the old

home, as Carl led them to the kitchen. It was a huge room, with an old, but obviously still working range and hood cover. Cooking utensils, large pots and pans and other cooking gadgets hung from the ceiling in handy groupings. In an apparent grudging concession to modern convenience, a walk in refrigerator/freezer combination stood against one wall.

"So what brings you back? Did my tales of the old, simpler days entice you?"

"In a way, yes," replied Victor. "My friends here were very interested in what I related about you. They were eager to hear more."

Carl frowned for a moment, unable to understand why they would drive all the way back up to Los Robles from Los Angeles just to hear about the old days from him. Still, not many listened to him anymore and a new audience might be just what he needed.

"All right," he said, passing out cups and pouring coffee, "let me tell you about it."

The three listened intently as Carl told about being born and raised in the Los Robles Valley, as had his grandfather and great grandfather before him. The McCormick's were ranchers, he told them, but at one time the family had owned the Los Robles Valley Railroad that had served so well during the twelve years of its existence. Wider, better highways and the coming of trucks had taken business away, though, and Carl's grandfather, "Engine Jack" McCormick, had sold the small steam engine and rolling stock to a railroad further north before shutting down his operation.

In the end, Carl told them, it didn't really matter since ranching produced more than enough income for anything "Engine Jack" wanted. In private, the man had admitted that the railroad was nothing more than a big toy for him that just happened to move cattle to the railhead connection on the coast, bringing feed and breeding stock back, in return. He often inviting selected cronies to join him on the round-trips, letting them blow the whistle and take the controls.

Carl's great grandfather, "Whispering McCormick", had started the family presence in the valley, when he took on the job as stage driver. Years of yelling at the horses as he urged them over the pass to San Ramon eventually led him to the affectionate nickname he became stuck with. He started the ranch in 1890 and watched it grow from a few acres near the Rio Tranquilo river to a respectable 5000 acre spread. He had encouraged his son, Jack, to build the railroad, but had declined to drive "that belching substitute for a horse." He died of natural causes at the age of seventy-five.

"Engine Jack" lived a quiet life, enjoying the valley and prospering. In 1954, though, at the age of seventy-one, his life changed as San Ramon began building a dam to create a reservoir to meet its growing water needs. At the same time, the city touted the money the campers and boaters would bring when they visited the adjoining recreational area.

Engine Jack's depth of anger over what the dam would do to the peaceful, isolated valley, in the words of his fellow old-time ranchers, "produced more steam and power than his little engine ever did!" Some of his friends openly voiced the opinion at his funeral a few years later, that "the damn dam did more to do him in at the age of 76," than any other event in his strong-willed life. "Engine Jack's" commitment to the valley and his fellow ranchers did not die with him – for his grandson, Carl, vowed to carry on.

Carl had been born in the same year his great grandfather "Whispering" had died. Eleven years later, his father, Jack, Jr., was killed in North Africa serving with Patton. "Engine Jack" had always been like a second father to Carl, and with the loss of Jack Jr., Grandfather and Grandson quickly developed strong ties to one another. While Carl's younger sister initially withdrew into her own shell, sticking close to her mother, the four of them eventually forged a McCormick family bond that buttressed them through the years.

While he was alive, "Engine Jack" constantly railed against the dam. He saw it as San Ramon's knife at the heart of the valley. He thoroughly resented the city's power over the county government, exploiting the rural, simple character of the land and its people for their own purposes.

Carl too, had watched with disgust as the dam was completed. At the time, two things happened that forever shaped his sentiments: his mother died after a short illness on the day it was dedicated; and, the next day, his sister had been thrown from her horse and died of a broken neck. She had been riding with Carl to look at the dried up streambed, cut off from the natural flow of water now that the dam's gates were closed.

The ensuing years and the large, growing lake had brought overwhelming crowds to the recreational area, clogging the roads throughout the valley. If that weren't enough, the visitors stayed on, buying homes and sending their kids into an unprepared, rural school system. And then they proceeded to tear up the local roads with their second cars and pickups, and now their SUVs.

Now, as Carl closed in on the end of his life – after all, hadn't his grandfather and great grandfather expired in their 70's? – he began developing an attitude about the "damn dam" and would often go up to the recreational area just to be near it and throw his energy at it, in desperate hope that it would go away.

"I must sound crazy to you," he said, hoping that he hadn't. "But, if you had lived here all your life and had seen that life change so dramatically because of the actions of others, well, I think you might end up feeling the same!"

"I can understand that," Clarene said softly. "I think it's basic human nature to resent that kind of intrusion. I even think that sending mental messages is very common and sometimes even works."

"But??...I feel like there's a great big 'BUT,' somehow coming after that. Is there?" Carl asked, hostilely.

"Yeah, I'm afraid there is," Clarene responded. "When the anger reaches a point that rational thought and behavior are overwhelmed by the desire to carry out destruction, then I think the person involved needs to be stopped."

"Just who is planning to carry out this destruction. And of what, may I ask? The dam??"

"You are. And yes, of the dam."

"Lady, are you crazy? How am I going to do that?"

"By blowing up the gates, of course, with the explosives you already have here on the ranch."

"I've seen some loonies in my time in this valley, lady. Most of them seem to come up on the weekends from L.A. You're no exception."

"I expected better than sarcasm from you, Carl."

"Carl, is it? We're not going to be that kind of friends. Call me Mr. McCormick and I'll call you...whatever comes to mind."

"I'll tell you what, *Carl*. Let's go through the details of what we know, and what we will go to the Sheriff with, if you don't stop this madness."

"Know?" Carl's facade of superiority faded for a moment as he stood up and walked to the sink to rinse his cup. "How do you know this? What are you, some kind of psychic?" His voice was contentious, sarcastic, belittling Clarene.

Victor's hand darted out to stop her reply, knowing it would be the wrong thing to say, but he was too late.

"As a matter of fact, I am. And a damn good one at that. Good enough to know what you're planning and good enough to track you down to stop it!"

Carl quietly clapped his hands in mock appreciation. "I guess that's supposed to intimidate me, huh?" he said, with a serious, deep voice. "Well, let me tell you something, I'm not impressed. Do you hear me? I'M NOT IMPRESSED!"

Before Clarene could say more, he continued. "And you know

why? For two reasons: one, I've thought about it, I admit that, but I haven't done anything about it; and, two, if you had all the facts that you imply you have, you would have gone to the Sheriff and he would be here, instead! No, lady, you're just playing a game of some sort and I don't want a part of it."

Clarene glared at him. "We're in this game, as you call it, whether you want us to be, OR NOT!" She almost screamed the words at him, her temper matching her red hair. "Let me tell you what we know, so you don't go underestimating us any further. We know that you have the dynamite in one of those buildings out there along the road. We know that you've figured out how to explode it underwater by putting it in waterproof drums and sinking them next to the gates. We know you're going to set them off early in the morning. And what's worse, we know the amount of destruction you're going to cause by your callous disregard for all the people downstream."

"Listen to yourself, lady," Carl retorted. "First you say I'm gonna put the dynamite in waterproof drums and then I'm going to sink them next to the gates. If the drums sink in the water, the dynamite will get all wet and can't work. Your theory is laughable."

"Not if you use double drums, a smaller one inside the outer one. The inside drum will protect and concentrate the explosion and the outer one can be drilled with holes so it can be sunk. Sunk where you want by guiding it from above with a rope."

Carl looked at her with new appreciation. "One drum setup wouldn't be enough to blow up the gates on that dam!"

"Of course, not. That's why you're planning to use three." The images of him building the drums and sinking them next to the gates were vivid in her mind.

Carl settled back into the kitchen chair, closely observing Clarene. "So, how do I set them off?"

"Carl, Carl, you know how; you bought three timers. Simple timers that you'll hook to batteries that will send a current to the blasting caps that you'll hook to the dynamite. All you have to do is set the timers with enough time to sink the drums and get away before anyone sees you in the early morning."

"Great plan!" he replied with vigor. "I think it's foolproof." He then eyed her very strongly, adding, "Sounds to me, like it's something you plan to do yourselves and then set me up to take the blame."

Pointing at Victor, he continued his angry accusation. "He was up here yesterday, looking for caves for some reason, and later when we were talking he mentioned that the only way left to get to them, would be to drop the water level." Turning to Victor, he said, "Remember that? It was *you* who said the way to get to the caves was to drop the water level."

"I was just talking, I didn't mean we were going to do it." Victor was still flustered over the results of *that* conversation and didn't want to hear anymore about it.

"What's in the caves that you want so badly, hmmm? Buried treasure? If you go back far enough in the history of this valley, sooner or later you come across the stories of buried treasure. There are stories of maps and gold and the disappearance of the daughter of the Comandante of Monterey. Is that what you're all after? I bet it is and I bet my close friend Sheriff Rodriguez will be very interested to hear what you have planned."

Clarene was astonished at how successfully Carl had turned the tables on her, putting her and the others on the defensive. She tried to think of how she could convince him to stop his plans, but he pre-empted her.

"I think it's time for you all to go. I welcomed you in my home and offered you my hospitality and then you accuse me of planning to do vile things. You've told me all kinds of things I didn't need or want to know, and now that I know how to blow up the dam – because you've told me – you're threatening to go to the Sheriff. That's absurd!"

He stopped for a moment, eyed Clarene with old, but bright eyes and then added, "Do your best, lady, but I doubt Roberto will believe you."

"Roberto?"

"Yeah, as is Sheriff Rodriguez. Now, please leave."

Clarene, Janice and Victor awkwardly extracted themselves from the kitchen, tracing their steps back to the front porch and then to the Blazer. Carl stood defiantly in the doorway, holding the screen door ajar as he watched them turn around at the front of the house and drive down the long driveway back to the road to town.

Once outside the entrance to the ranch, Clarene screeched her frustration, slapping her hand on the dash. "That man is impossible! Let's find the Sheriff's station and report him!"

"For what? Throwing us out of his house?" Victor could be calm now that Clarene had taken the lead in being angry.

"For being an Adam Henry!" Clarene was furious, her voice steady but shrill.

"A what?" Janice hadn't heard that term before.

"An ass-hole. That's the code term Bill and his fellow Deputies use."

Janice smiled. Victor laughed.

But, Clarene wasn't laughing with them. She grabbed the map, unfolded it with determination and then began searching for an icon that indicated where the Sheriff's station was located. She was not gentle with the map, but soon located what she sought and gave Victor directions on how to find the place.

The Sheriff's office was in the middle of a block of small shops and businesses; it was marked only with a large symbol of a badge over the door and the American and State Flags out in front.

Victor pulled the Blazer into one of the angled parking spaces in front and got out. Clarene jumped out and beat him to the sidewalk. With nose flared and red-hair screaming its warning for casual pedestrians to stay out of the way, she grabbed the handle of the glass door and jerked it open. She was on her way to a close encounter of her own kind.

The officer behind the desk saw her and stood up, bracing

himself mentally and physically for this charging woman with a full head of steam.

"Is Sheriff Rodriguez in?" she demanded.

"Yes ma'am. Can I tell him what it's about?"

"I want to prevent a crime."

The officer excused himself and walked towards the back of the station and into a small office. She could hear enough of the conversation from where she stood at the front counter to know that Carl had already called and warned his friend about her.

She heard the Sheriff tell the deputy to get rid of her, but Clarene quickly put a stop to that nonsense by walking around the counter and back to Rodriguez's office, herself. Once there, she eased the deputy aside, and with hands on her shapely hips, spoke directly to Captain Roberto Rodriguez, of the San Ramon County Sheriff's Department.

"I take it Carl McCormick has already called you."

"Yes. Said you were a nut intent on blowing up the dam and blaming him for it."

"You *can't* believe that. Do I look like a person who would blow up the dam?"

"Ma'am, there are no known profiles or images of people who are prone to blow up dams. We're an equal opportunity Sheriff's Department and you can qualify yourself for that job as easily as anyone else."

"Are you trying to be funny?"

"I'm very serious, ma'am."

Clarene stopped for a moment in her headlong dash to disaster and regrouped her thoughts. Rodriguez just starred at her, waiting.

"I'm sorry I got off on the wrong foot here. I work with the Los Angeles County Sheriff's Department . . ."

"You're a Deputy?"

"No. But I work closely with them, as I'm sure they'll be happy to tell you."

"Work closely with them?" His eyes widened and his eyebrows turned up in disbelief. "In what capacity?"

"I do forensic analysis."

"Meaning?"

Clarene tried to remain calm, for the next few sentences she uttered would determine the kind of support she would get from this Sheriff.

"I have some very special abilities that they have found useful over the last eight years in solving homicides and other heinous crimes. I have also had the privilege of working with the FBI on several occasions in the same manner."

"Special abilities? FBI? Lady, Carl said you were nuts and I'm inclined to believe him. Now, why don't you just leave quietly and I'll forget you were here. And, the reason I'm being so generous is because it would takes me hours, if not days, to fill out all the paperwork involved in arresting you for terrorist activities."

"Terrorist activities?" Clarene's temper started to boil again. All the emotions and all of the frustration she had acquired over the last week in trying to stop the destruction that she knew was coming, welled up and spewed forth at Sheriff Rodriguez. "Let me tell you about terrorist activities!"

Twenty minutes later, a very weary Rodriguez slumped in his chair, overwhelmed with the depth and vehemence of her tale. Eventually, he inhaled a deep breath, looked Clarene in the eye and said slowly, "Ma'am, I don't know what you've been eating lately, but I strongly suggest you change your diet. Try very bland foods. If you drink, stop. If you like horror films or books, stay away from them." His voice getting stronger, he went on, "There is no way in hell I am going to take you seriously, or even think about acting on your accusations. Carl McCormick is a long time resident of this valley and enjoys the respect of this office and his neighbors. I have a nice job here, and I expect to retire from here in another five years. I do not, repeat, DO NOT want to go into my last years before retirement with a big sign around my neck saying "kick me, I believed a psychic!"

He stood up and walked towards her, reaching for her elbow. "Now, please, get out of here and don't come back!"

* * *

Clarene was furious with the Sheriff for being so condescending and with herself for being unable to convince him of what she knew was about to happen. Making no attempt to control her anger, she grabbed her cell phone from her purse and pushed a memory button. Moments later Bill Edwards was on the line.

"Bill, this is Clarene," she shouted. "That idiot Sheriff of yours up here won't believe me and threw me out of his office!"

"He's not my Sheriff; I've never met him. And, if you were yelling at him like you're yelling at me, I can see why."

"Why are you saying that?" she demanded. After all the years of working so closely with him and his people, she had expected nothing but full support.

Assuming his best authority-laden voice, Bill answered her bluntly. "Listen to me, Clarene, you're out of your element. Down here, working with us, you're respected, but up there, in the boonies, you're just another big city nut. Down here, you have your Institute and are loved and have all kinds of people coming to see you and get readings. They believe in you and know, from experience, that what you tell them is going to happen. Up there, you're just another big city nut, the kind of nut that fakes her way through life making up phony predictions.

"I would bet a million bucks you ignored my recommendations about gathering hard evidence and facts and, instead, just went charging in there, full of emotion with nothing but your premonitions to back you up! That's what happened, isn't it? That's why he threw you out!"

"No. We went to Carl's ranch. We were in his kitchen! We drove past the barns where he's making the explosives! I know what I felt and sensed as we drove in, I know he's doing it!"

"That's not enough, Clarene! You're in my world now, and we deal in facts, not fantasy."

"It's not fantasy, and you know it!"

"Look Clarene, I believe in you, but how do I get it across to you that that doesn't mean jack shit when you're trying to deal with decision-makers outside your cloistered circle of friends and believers! Now, listen to me and do as I tell you. Get evidence, get facts, get information that can be touched, felt, seen. Create the trail leading from one point to another, so that Sheriff Rodriguez has to act."

Clarene exhaled slowly as the message settled in and her anger began to dissolve. "All right, I'll see what we can do."

"That's great, Clarene. Just don't break any laws doing it."

"What laws could we break?"

"Those against trespass, assault, theft, filing false reports and slander, just to name a few."

She was stunned. "For God's sake, help me then! I need you here!"

"I can't get there!"

"Why not. Take some time off. I'd do the same for you, if you needed help – and you know it!"

"It's not the time, I haven't got any wheels. You've got my Blazer, remember?"

"Use Victor's Volvo."

"Clarene, the real reason he didn't want to use the Volvo when he went up there on Friday, was because it probably wouldn't have made it. And it probably won't make it now, either."

"Oh." She paused, thinking of a way around the problem. "Then call Sheriff Rodriguez, tell him about me and the work I do for your Department. Throw lots of laurels at me, do whatever you have to, but get him to believe me!"

"I can't do that, Clarene. No matter how much I personally believe in you, I can't do that."

"WHY NOT?"

"Because I'm a Deputy Sheriff and department policy prevents me from using my position that way. As soon as I tell Rodriguez that I'm with the Los Angeles County Sheriff's Department and that I work with you, everything else I say takes on the mantle of authority of this office. And, this office is not involved with the matter. It doesn't involve us or any of our jurisdictions. Damnit, Clarene, you're asking me to put my job on the line and I can't do that, no matter how much I believe in your premonitions! Now, do as I said earlier, get the facts. Go and GET THE FRIGGIN' FACTS!"

* * *

Victor was breathing heavily. He wasn't used to climbing over fence rails and crouching and crawling through tall grass – not with his potbelly. He had parked the Blazer on the road some ways away from the entrance to Carl's ranch, so as not to draw attention. Now he was heading for the barn-like building Clarene had identified as the place where the explosives were being assembled.

Clarene and Janice had stayed with the car, trying to act like tourists by holding the map and looking interested in the rural atmosphere. How long they could pull that off was questionable, but it was the best they could come up with under the circumstances.

Victor reached the barn unseen and finding an open side door, eased himself inside. It was long and wide, full of empty horse stalls and the smell of moist hay randomly scattered about the floor. At the far end, just inside a set of high double sliding doors, he saw the three drums sitting on a series of sawhorses. He could see light coming through some holes in one of them, but the others seemed untouched.

Getting closer, he peered into the first one and found that it contained a smaller inner drum held in place by brackets. Inside, he saw what appeared to be a timer of some sort with wires extended, but unconnected. He looked around for the dynamite, but saw none.

The sound of an approaching vehicle caused him to jerk around, looking for a quick escape, but the only way out, other than the double doors, was the way he'd come in. He moved quickly toward the side door and crouched in a recess as the double doors at the opposite end rumbled open. Victor feared the worst that Carl had found him, but the man in the doorway was shorter, younger, heavier than Carl; a ranch hand going about his business. He was in and out quickly, never even looking at the other end where the drums stood on the sawhorses.

Victor couldn't see what the guy had picked up, but it didn't matter. He was gone and now Victor was too.

FIFTEEN

Monday Morning

The three spent the night in Los Robles, knowing they had to stay close to Carl, keeping watch as best they could, while trying to get the evidence they needed to convince the Sheriff to act.

After finding a motel, they had eaten dinner, then returned in the twilight to Carl's ranch to watch for activity. In the fading sunlight they could see the lights in the barn were on. The distant sounds of sporadic pounding and grinding of metal wafted towards them on the evening breeze, but they couldn't know for sure what was going on behind the walls.

Victor volunteered to sneak up to the barn again; but, it was growing darker and he knew from his first foray, that the ground was uneven and contained numerous hazards in the form of large rocks, pointy stumps and lots of cattle droppings. Under the circumstances, he had been easily talked out of the venture in favor of waiting for the light of dawn.

With the arrival of the new day, the three of them, rested and fed, drove out once more on the now familiar streets and roads to Carl's ranch and parked on the shoulder. Victor got out, told

Clarene to drive away so the Blazer wouldn't be seen in the area, and to come back to pick him up in about a half-hour.

He was already over the fence as she pulled back onto the road and left.

Retracing his route, Victor stealthily reached the barn and entered again through the side door. The morning light at the end of the barn highlighted the three drums perched on the sawhorses. The light streaming through the holes in each yelled the story of what Carl had done the night before.

Victor walked over to them and peered inside, holding his bifocals up on his nose with two fingers to keep them from falling off. Each now had a smaller inner drum centered in place with brackets, each containing the same sort of timer he had seen yesterday in the first one. The holes in the large outer drums, the size and shape of used 55 gallon oil drums, had been drilled with a circular hole cutter, such as the kind used to put holes in doors for handles and locks. The metal of the outer drums must have been very tough, for there were many used blades scattered nearby on the floor.

Victor counted at least twelve holes around the sides of each drum, and as he stared inside at the construction of the explosive mechanisms, he noticed three more holes drilled in each bottom. It was easy to picture how easily the devices would be sunk in place after being carried by boat to the desired location. Carl would only have to roll each over the side and guide them into place with ropes. The drums would not be heavy, only awkward, and once filled with water, would shape and concentrate the force of the inner-drum explosions on the gates and their supporting columns with destructive efficiency.

Victor looked again for the dynamite that he was sure Carl would use, but failed to find it. If it was in the barn, it was hidden. Victor sensed that it wasn't, though. Carl was no dummy, he had to assume that Clarene might convince someone of his intentions and as long as the dynamite and the drums weren't together, it would be hard to prove his intentions. No, Carl could assemble the explosive packages separately and then merely insert the connecting wires to the timers before sealing the tops of the inner drums at the drop point. It was a matter of simple construction, simple assembly, and simple application.

Fearing a repeat of yesterday's intrusion by the ranch hand, Victor took a quick last look for any other obvious evidence and seeing none, exited the side door. Had he looked back as he hurriedly crept through the grass on his way back to the road, he might have seen the glint of the morning sun off the binoculars pointed at him from the front upstairs bedroom in the main house.

He waited only a few moments before Clarene arrived to pick him up.

"Well?" she demanded. The night's rest and beauty of the rural morning had not lessened her determination to stop the madness. "What did you find?"

"He's got three bombs under construction. Pretty much the way you described them. They're very close to being complete, if not already done..."

"So, he can blow the dam up anytime he wants, now?" Clarene interrupted.

Victor ignored her outburst. "I wasn't able to see any dynamite around, so he's probably got that hidden elsewhere. When he's ready for it, he'll have to do some things to make it work, like tying it together in a bundle and inserting blasting caps. That won't take much time, though; in fact, maybe he's done that already."

"So he *can* blow up the dam anytime he wants?" Clarene repeated her question, this time as a statement.

"That's a possibility."

Janice, who had remained quiet for most of the trip, now startled them with a question. "Why don't we go back and steal them? If he doesn't have them, how can he blow them up?"

The simple clarity of the idea was overwhelming.

"Why not?" Victor replied enthusiastically. "If we succeed,

he has to start over, and we have hard evidence of what he was doing and planning."

"Remember what Bill said," Clarene interjected. "If we get caught, we could be charged with trespass and theft."

"I doubt, if we get caught, that Carl will want to press charges with all the publicity it would entail. If the story were to get out that he was somehow involved in planning to blow up the dam, he could never try it again, for he would always be the prime suspect. No, I think stealing the bombs *is* a good idea. It's a win-win situation for us."

Clarene started to reply, but was startled to hear the quick burp of the blare horn behind her. Looking in the mirror, she saw the red lights of the Sheriff's patrol car. "Pull over, lady," the voice coming from the loudspeaker mounted in its grill was firm and authoritative.

She drove the Blazer to the nearest space and stopped.

She could see two uniformed officers in the car. Clarene didn't recognize the driver, but the burley, older man getting out the passenger side was Sheriff Rodriguez. He straightened his holster belt and he walked purposefully around the back of the Blazer towards Clarene on the driver's side.

"Had a busy morning, have we?" he asked.

"Excuse me?" Clarene responded, acting innocent.

"You know, for a bunch of psychics, you guys are inept. Now, up here, we tend to run our lives in a less sophisticated, slower manner than you do down there in the great, smog-laden land of the lotus. But, there are a few things we do adhere to. We don't go where we're not wanted, nor invited. And, we don't break into other people's homes or property. Both of those are kinda big no-no's." He starred at Clarene, challenging her to respond.

When she didn't, he went on. "I got a call a bit ago, says your buddy there," pointing at Victor, "was trespassing on Carl's ranch. Seems he broke into one of his barn's."

Looking straight out the front window, Victor said nothing, trying to ignore the Sheriff.

"So, here's what we're going to do, people," he said with purpose. "You're going to follow me down to the station – you know where that is, of course – and we're going to talk about the charges I'm going to file against you."

"Charges? Are you going to arrest us?" Clarene's voice climbed higher as her adrenaline began pumping.

"Yes. For trespass and breaking and entering."

"Good. Do it!" she blurted out. "That suits me just fine. That will put the whole thing out on the table. And, while you're at it, let's call the newspapers and the television stations, too. I've got a big following in Los Angeles and I'm sure the reporters will all want to hear my story. You can make front page headlines!"

"Headlines? About what?" Rodriguez asked, sarcastically. "That some nut from L.A. is up here making accusations against one of our leading citizens? That she hasn't got a shred of evidence to support her crazy assumptions? That I've already warned her once, and in spite of that warning has perpetrated two misdemeanors on the property of said leading citizen?"

"We have evidence!"

"Show me!"

"I can't."

"Then it ain't evidence, lady. It ain't evidence."

"It would be, if you looked at it yourself. If you saw and touched it, then it would be evidence, wouldn't it?"

"And, how is that going to come about?"

"Come with us, we'll go back to the ranch and show you."

"Just what part of the Constitution regarding search and seizure don't you understand? I'm a law officer; I have to follow the law. I have to have probable cause, supported by facts, not conjecture. And, I have to have a search warrant. I don't have the first, so I sure as hell won't be getting the other. Even if I believed you, which I don't, I would have to convince a Judge, which I couldn't, considering the person involved."

He paused for a moment to gather his breath and summon a final warning and order. "I don't need this aggravation, the city of Los Robles doesn't need the aggravation, and neither does Carl McCormick. I will let you go and not file any charges, if you agree to leave town and drop this silly crusade! And, I mean now!"

The look on his face was stony, determined, and well practiced. It could overwhelm even the heartiest aggressive behavior.

Clarene saw it differently. She took the measure of Captain Roberto Rodriguez as he faced her and found she had won. There would be no charges filed, no arrests made. Victor had been right, Carl didn't want this out in the open and the Sheriff didn't want the embarrassment. While the Sheriff didn't believe her story, he did know Carl well enough to realize he might be capable of such an act. Clarene sensed he knew first hand about Carl's hatred of the dam.

She nodded at Rodriguez in acknowledgment of his commands, but did not give him the satisfaction of saying so. She merely started the Blazer and slowly drove away as the Sheriff stood back and then returned to his cruiser.

"I want those bombs!" Clarene exclaimed. "Let's get them now, before Carl has a chance to move them!" She made a quick U-turn, ignoring the Sheriff's cruiser, and headed the Blazer back towards Carl's ranch. Once there, she brazenly drove up the driveway and stopped in front of the barn. She jumped out, ran around to the back of the green SUV and opened the lid of the rear cargo area, shoving it upwards the last few inches when it failed to move fast enough to suit her. Leading the way, with Victor and Janice just behind, she slid open the large double doors and marched inside, determined to grab the drums and run.

But, they were nowhere to be seen. The sawhorses were gone. The used hole blades were gone. There was nothing but hay and horses. "Are you sure this is the right barn?" she demanded of Victor.

"Of course, it is!" he answered. "He must have beat us to them. He's taken them and we're too late!"

Thwarted once again, Clarene and Victor began to feel a bit

of panic as they rushed about the huge barn, looking for any clue that might help them find Carl. Their frustration grew stronger with each passing, unproductive second – until Janice interjected herself with the voice of youthful wisdom, "Why don't you guys relax and your use abilities to find him?"

"Huh?" Victor looked at her, quizzically.

"I'm trying to say that you should relax for a few moments, then use your sensory abilities to figure this out. You both have gotten so wrapped up in this that it seems like your egos have taken over. At least, that's what it looks like to me. So, I think it might be good if you both stepped back from it for a bit and let whatever flows inside you, start to flow and work for you. I mean, how do you do it back at the Institute, when there's no pressure on? I think that's what you have to do here."

Clarene shook her head in amazement, recognizing the truth when she heard it. She and Victor had once again let their egos dominate the situation, undermining the senses they both could have employed. She mouthed a personal 'thank you' to Janice and taking Victor by the hand, headed back for the double doors and the Blazer.

The glaring light of the morning sun blocked their vision for a moment as they emerged from the shadowed interior of the barn. When they were able to stop squinting, the Sheriff's Cruiser, parked in a way so as to block the Blazer's escape, came into full focus. Sheriff Rodriguez and his deputy stood nearby, handcuffs at the ready. "I warned you, lady. Now, you're all under arrest for trespass and illegal entry. Please turn around."

He cuffed them, placed them in the back seat of the Cruiser and hurried back to the Sheriff's station. Once inside, he led them to the holding cell.

"What about our car?" demanded Clarene, voice climbing, as her cuffs were removed.

"It'll be towed."

"Where?" A nervous twitch started in her left wrist and worked its way down her hand and fingers.

"To the lot, about four blocks from here, where they're kept. You'll get it back, but it'll cost you money for towing and storage. Is it registered in your name?"

"What difference does that make?"

"Because only the registered owner can claim and retrieve it."

"It's not mine."

"Stolen?"

"Of course, not. It's belongs to a friend of mine."

"I'll need his name and number."

"His name is Bill Edwards. I don't remember his number. I usually call him with the automatic dialer on my phone."

"Well you better let him know, somehow. Also, you better call your Attorney. You're going to need one."

"For a couple of misdemeanors? We'll just pay some fines and walk. That is, if you can make the charges stick!"

"I can, lady. I can. Remember, it was me and the deputy that were there, we both saw you. The charges will stick."

Clarene's bravado, coupled with her limited knowledge of the law were becoming a hindrance. Dejected, she sat on the bench in the holding cell and reached for her phone. But her purse was on the Sheriff's desk, where he taken it after removing it from her.

"I need my phone," she called out. Moments passed before she sensed the game in progress. "Pleeassse," she added.

Rodriguez ambled in and slowly extended his hand, giving her the phone. He was smirking.

As she took it from him, it finally dawned on her that she was in a terrible situation, one for which her vaunted psychic abilities had not prepared her. She had overplayed her hand, with the wrong guy, at the wrong time. There was only one thing left to do – call Bill Edwards.

* * *

"I warned you Clarene. I told you to be careful and not break the law!" Bill was not a happy Deputy; not a happy Deputy, at all. Not only was his favorite psychic in jail, but so were Janice and Victor, and in a way, his car, too. "What are you being charged with?"

"As I said," Clarene responded from the holding cell, "he says it's trespass and illegal entry. He also said he was adding something about failing to heed a lawful order of a peace officer."

"What's the basis for that?"

"He told us twice to drop the matter and get out of town."

"That's got some holes, but it'll do. What's really bad about all this, is that you've been stopped from watching that McCormick guy. Now you can't see where he's going and what he's doing. You say he's got the bombs almost finished?"

"Yes. As far as I know from what we've seen and from what our senses tell us, Carl has taken the bombs. I'd say he was going to put them in place tomorrow morning and blow them up!"

There was no response.

"Damnit, Bill!" Clarene yelled into the phone as she stood up, pacing the floor of the cell. "He's going to get away with it and we're sitting here on our butts in jail, unable to stop him! You've got to help me. You know it's going to happen and we're powerless. Do something!"

There was no response.

"Bill? Bill are you there?"

"Hang on." It wasn't so much a command, as it was a 'be quiet, you're interrupting something.' In the background she heard mumbled voices deep in conversation. Then a hand at the other end covered the mouthpiece, forcing her to wait.

A few moments later there was the sound of fingers adjusting their hold on the distant mouthpiece, allowing her to hear a muffled, but angry voice telling Bill, "she's got us in a fine pickle! If we don't back her, we'll never be able to use her again; her credibility will be shot to hell! And wait until the news media guys get on this. They'll have a field day with her, and us, too! We'll all look like a bunch of friggin' idiots! Damnit all to hell, Bill, she doesn't give us any choice. We've got to get involved, just to protect ourselves and our reputations after having used her all these years!" There was a brief pause and then a final commitment to reality. "We just don't have any choice, Bill. Tell her we'll be there this afternoon. I'll get a chopper to take us."

Clarene could hardly contain her elation. The smile on her face spread to her cellmates as she mouthed "he's coming, with his boss." Then she held her finger up to her lips. Rodriguez needn't know that, for now.

SIXTEEN

Monday Morning

After calling in the report that Victor was breaking into his barn, Carl had quickly taken action to remove and conceal his work from any further possibility of discovery.

It was a warm morning, and the same ranch hand that Victor had seen the day before, was already sweating from helping Carl load the 55 gallon drums into the back of a power boat. The boat was strapped down to a trailer that was hitched to the back of Carl's brown pickup, and was parked near the barn. He hadn't seen the boat around the ranch before, so he figured Carl had borrowed it from one of his cronies. It was a beautiful, sleek craft with a pointed bow and powerful, twin outboards that he knew would thrust it through the water at unbelievable speeds. He hoped he would be invited to go along for a ride.

The drums were awkward, but not heavy. He and Carl easily lifted each of the three and placed them in the rear of the boat on the left side. Each was tied with a rope arrangement, like a big version of that used on a hanging basket, which led to a single long rope coiled on top of each drum.

"What are you going to do with these, Mr. Carl?" he asked.

"I'm going fishing!"

"Fishing? That sounds good. Where?"

"At the lake."

"They don't allow no fishing at that lake!"

"I know. That's why I made these things. They're big fish traps. The fish go in the holes on the sides and then are so dumb they can't get out. When I pull the barrels back up, I'll have me a lot of fine fish." Carl hadn't hired the man for his intelligence; he'd been hired because he knew how to do ranch work without a lot of supervision. It made Carl feel superior talking down to him.

"Are you going fishing today?"

"No. But, I'll leave pretty soon – just as soon as we're done. I'll take the rest of today to get organized. Then, I'll spend the night up there so I can get up early in the morning; you know, before it gets light. That way, I can get these fish traps lowered into place before anyone sees me. Tomorrow night we'll have ourselves a dinner of the finest fish in the lake. Nice fat fish, that have just been waiting for me to catch them!"

When they finished with the drums, the man started to reach for a big, metal toolbox that had been sitting on the ground. Carl quickly grabbed it, though, and put it in the boat up front by the driver's seat. He covered it with a couple of large rags and then walked to the backside of the boat to cover the three drums with a section of canvas tarp.

Surveying the results of his work, Carl nodded his head in pleasure. Waving good-bye, he got in the truck and headed towards the front entrance of the ranch and the highway leading to the dam. It was just past ten o'clock in the morning.

* * *

Monday Afternoon

At the jail, Clarene and the others were fed a sparse lunch at county expense and waited impatiently for Bill and his Captain to arrive. She had no idea how long it would take and where they would land. All she knew was that Carl was totally free to do his thing and that she was powerless to stop him. After all the frustration she had endured in trying to find out who was going to blow up the dam, it seemed the ultimate irony to have blocked herself from keeping him from doing it.

She was furious with herself and even more furious with Sheriff Rodriguez for being so...so...so self-centered and unenlightened about the possibility of her telling the truth about Carl and his plans.

She tried to relax, tried to take Janice's advice about letting her inner thoughts come to the surface, but failed.

She had never encountered a situation like this before, where she was so personally and totally involved. Her experiences in helping people were based on the ability to view things about them at a distance. She hadn't let the emotions of a situation draw her in to the extent it had this time, clouding her abilities. A whole new set of rules were being applied; rules she didn't know how to play by. It was confusing to her, for under some circumstances she could 'read' the energy and her senses would give her directions to follow. But then, just as easily, her ego would kick in with full fury and destroy her abilities to find further leads.

She chided herself over and over. Obviously, there was something in all this that she had to learn. Patience was certainly one of the lessons. But, more important, was the lesson that she was, after all, only human. She was *not* the right hand of justice. She had not been anointed to save all the people downstream from death and disaster.

That was an easy enough decision for her rational mind, but

then her ego fought back, demanding that she still pursue attention and results. It took a few hours of agitated argument within herself, but she finally gained control and was able to ignore the ego.

When she was done, Clarene sat down on the bench in the holding cell and looked at her two compatriots. "It will resolve itself."

Victor was amazed at her statement and started to question her meaning, but Sheriff Rodriguez distracted him by coming over from his office.

"We'll have you out of here in a little while. We're going to transfer you down to the main jail in San Ramon, where they will formally book and fingerprint you. Tomorrow morning you'll appear before a judge to enter pleas and have bail set. As I suggested before, you will probably want to get legal counsel. I also have to warn you that the booking process is not a pleasant one, especially for the uninitiated. You will go through a strip search with all those probing fingers and you will be issued inmate uniforms. Make up your mind now not to fight it. Those guards down there won't take any crap from anyone and they just love it when new inmates resist. Any questions?"

"Yes." Clarene was horrified at the thought, but unwilling to give him the pleasure of showing it. "What about the car?" she asked, instead.

"I think I told you. It's been towed into storage. The owner will have to pay for the towing and the storage fee to get it out, if he can prove he owns it."

Clarene knew it was the right time to tell Rodriguez about Bill.

"The owner is a Deputy Sheriff with the Los Angeles County Sheriff's Department. He's the guy I told you about yesterday, that I work with in solving homicide cases. He's coming up with his Captain – to talk to you."

"Talk to me? Why?"

"They know me and have worked with me for several years. I'm reliable and when I give them leads they always pan out."

"So you give them names and addresses of killers, huh?"

"No. I give them information and descriptions and leads to follow that aren't readily apparent to normal investigation techniques. I can scratch a bit deeper and come up with leads that aren't visible to the naked eye. They take it from there. We have a huge success rate in closing difficult cases."

"So, you were doing some work for them and decided Carl McCormick was a likely suspect for some unsolved crime?"

"No. That's not it, at all." Clarene was doing very well in controlling her ego and its manifest desire to reach through the bars and choke the stupid son-of-a-bitch on the other side. "But," she calmly continued, "Carl McCormick *is* a likely perpetrator of a crime in progress, a crime you can yet prevent."

"Yeah, you tried to hook me with that garbage yesterday. You had a dream and then another and then another. All of them about the dam being blown up, all of them grabbing and leading you to Carl McCormick! We've covered all this, lady. It won't fly."

Clarene looked at him and smiled, a smile that she knew from experience could melt the heart of her worst critics on TV talk shows. "I'll tell you what," she said, softly, "give me 15 minutes alone with you in your office and I'll change your mind."

Rodriguez screwed up his face in a maze of questions and concern. Just what did she have in mind, he wondered? Would he be safe? Was she going to try and inflict the untold pleasures of the east on him to change his mind? *What the hell,* he thought, *I'm getting old and there's no time like the present. The only question is, do I send the deputy away or do I keep him around in case I need help?*

In the end, he left the deputy at the front desk, always in view while he listened to Clarene behind closed doors. At the end of the fifteen minutes, Captain Roberto Rodriguez, like Bill's Captain in Bellflower, was a convert – dubious as to how she did it, but a convert, nonetheless.

As he reopened the door to his office, the deputy got up and walked over with a note in hand. "Just got a radio call from a L.

A. Sheriff's Office helicopter. They're inbound to the Los Robles Valley airport and requested that we send a car to meet them."

Clarene looked at her watch. She wondered how much time was left before the van would arrive to take them to San Ramon. It could be tight, but it looked to her like things were going to work out, yet!

Rodriguez handed the note back to the Deputy. "All right, get out there and bring them in."

Twenty minutes later the deputy arrived back at the station from the small valley airport where the LASO chopper had landed with Bill and his Captain. He parked the cruiser next to the Sheriff's transfer van, already in a space by the front door.

Waving to the Deputy standing by the van, he opened the door for the two visitors and pointed towards Rodriguez's office in the rear.

Clarene made introductions. She started to join them as the three men retired to Rodriguez's office, but was eased aside by Bill as they entered the door. The deputy who had driven them from the airport returned to his chair at the front desk. From there, he could see by the animated conversations and smiling faces that the meeting was going well.

It had been going on for about twenty minutes when the deputy driving the transfer van suddenly opened the front door and shoved a man through, in front of him.

"I think you need to hear what this guy has to say," he said.

"What's up?" asked the deputy behind the desk.

"Says he thinks his boss has gone nuts. Says he thinks he's gone up to some dam and lake around here to go fishing with barrels filled with explosives!"

"Holy shit!" The deputy jumped up and ran to Rodriguez's office and threw the door open without knocking.

"Guy out front says his boss is on his way to the lake to go fishing with barrels filled with explosives!" His voice was tense, direct.

"Show the guy in!" Rodriguez barked, as he jumped up from his seat.

The deputy ran back to the front door and grabbed the man by his arm and ushered him through the station to the Captain's office.

Rodriguez was brusque and to the point. "Who are you? Why do you think your boss has gone to the lake to go fishing with explosives?"

"You know me," the man said, removing his old, battered cowboy hat, "I work for Mr. Carl at the ranch." He was shaking at the knees and his words were stammered.

"All right, calm down. I'm sorry I jumped at you," Rodriguez said in a tranquil voice. "I recognize you now. What's going on? Why do you think he's got explosives and going to the lake?"

"I helped him load some barrels, you know, some 55 gallon drums, into the back of a boat. They had holes in them and he said he was going to go fishing with them." The words were jumbled together in a rush to get out.

"Take it easy," Rodriguez said again. "Take a deep breath and give it to us slowly. Where are the explosives? In the barrels?"

"I don't think so."

"Then where?" Rodriguez was getting impatient. He wanted answers.

Bill stood up and walked over to him and said, "Look, we know you have a good reason for coming here, so take your time and let it out. I know you must have thought about what to say on your way over here, so tell us about it."

The man *had* thought about what he would say and why, and with a moment's break, proceeded to let it out. He told them about helping to load the drums in the boat; about how fast and sleek it was; about having seen the drums in the barn while Mr. Carl built them; about wondering why there was an inner drum and why the outer drums all had holes in them. He had been curious, but he knew his boss did peculiar things at times and let it go at that. It wasn't until later, when he had gone to the locker where the dynamite was kept, that he found that it was gone. He was going to use some of it to try and get rid of a tree stump in the old creek bed, but the locker was empty.

After he had finished helping Mr. Carl to load the boat, he had started thinking about it and decided the old man was going up to the lake to blow up the fish just for the fun of it. Mr. Carl didn't like to eat fish; he was a beef man! He got worried about the old man's safety, worried that Mr. Carl might get wrapped up in the ropes when he put the drums over the side, or do some other stupid thing and really get hurt. He was genuinely concerned for the man's safety and that overcame all his other concerns about tattling on his boss. He just *had* to come in and tell the Sheriff.

"Well, that pretty well wraps up your lady's theory," Rodriguez said to Bill. "I guess as long as you're here, you may as well help us. So, let's get our collective butts in gear and find this guy!"

"We've got our chopper standing by," Bill's Captain said. "We'll figure out about paying for the gas later, right now it's available, if you can get us back to it. We'll also need a map so we know where to go."

"My deputy will take care of getting you there. You can use the van outside. Forget the map. Take him with you when you go up. He can help coordinate our efforts. And, get your pilot to call in your radio frequencies. We'll need to be able to talk to you from the ground."

"Copy that, Captain," Bill said over his shoulder, as he headed for the front door. "All right, deputy," he called out, "let's go see if we can find this guy." He had just reached the front door with his Captain and the Deputy, when Clarene called out after them, "What about us? You can't just leave us here!"

"You and your two friends can stay here in my office, but you can't get involved," Rodriguez answered, moving to open the holding cell for Victor and Janice.

"Why? We're part of this!" she protested. "Victor and I can help find McCormick!"

"What happens if you get hurt?" Rodriguez growled. "What

happens if you get blown up? Not only will you be gone, but so will my retirement!"

"Believe me," Clarene pleaded, "we'll be all right. We've got to help, you have to let us go with you," She tried that look again on Rodriguez, but he wasn't having any of it this time. He was adamant.

Bill knew how she felt and intervened. "Look, Sheriff Rodriguez," he said, "I know where you're coming from and if I were in your position, I wouldn't let her come along, either. But, she's like a partner to me in these situations. We know how to talk to each other, how to communicate nuances that grow into leads. And, with Victor, her abilities are almost doubled and that's good for our side. This is an extraordinary situation and they've done a lot so far to help reveal the details. I think they're still important to helping us close it out and I'm asking that you reconsider her request. Please let her and the others be involved, you won't regret it."

Rodriguez looked around the group, counting facial votes. There were seven 'yeas' against his one 'no'. He reluctantly yielded, but not without the last word. "If any of you get hurt, I'll kill ya!"

* * *

The cruiser and the van left the station within moments of the other, the van on its way to the airport, the cruiser towards the lake. Both were Code 2, flashing lights, no siren, speeding, but not wanting to yell their presence and mission to those along the way. By the time the cruiser got to the entrance of the recreational area at the lake, the LASO helicopter was already nearby, its huge rotor blades thumping its presence for all to hear.

They would have plenty of time to find Carl, if he was there, for the summer daylight would keep the recreational area open to view for many more hours.

The first stop for Rodriguez was the admission gate to ask the attendant if he had seen McCormick and the boat. The attendant knew McCormick from his many visits to the lake and identified him as having arrived before noon. He knew he had gone down to the launch ramps, but didn't know where he had gone from there.

Rodriguez drove quickly to the area and found Carl's pickup truck parked in the lot with the boat trailer still attached. The boat, itself, though, was not to be seen.

"Edwards, this is Rodriguez," he called into his radio, ignoring call sign protocol. After all, the frequency was assigned to LASO and the nearest station for them was almost a hundred miles away. Fat chance he would be overheard.

"Go ahead, Captain." Bill replied.

"The boat has been launched and the suspect apparently is on board. Check out the lake and see if you see anything that looks like the speedboat the ranchhand described."

"10-4." The chopper veered away and started up the center of the lake.

Clarene and Victor walked to the edge of the water. Its deep blue surface was quickly blown into a choppiness as the helicopter passed over.

"He's hiding out there, somewhere, isn't he?" Victor said to her.

"Yes. It feels like he's up the lake somewhere in a cove, hidden by bushes and some trees. They won't see him from the air. I sense that he's just biding his time, hoping no one will follow; hoping we won't be able to convince anyone of what he intends to do."

"As soon as he sees that chopper, he'll know differently," Victor replied.

"Maybe. Remember it says Los Angeles Sheriff's Department

on the side, not San Ramon. He may get confused with that and consider he's all right."

"If would be better if they found him."

"It won't happen this afternoon, or even tonight. No, it'll be tomorrow morning. He has to come out then, if he's going to have any chance of succeeding. Remember, too, my first dream showed an early morning scene at the dam. I'm sure it will all come down to stopping him tomorrow morning."

"That makes sense. Should we tell Rodriguez?" Victor asked.

"No, let's let him keep the pressure on, just as if we weren't here."

"Can *I* say something?" Janice interjected. She had been awfully quiet and suddenly found herself with an urge to say something important.

"Of course, Janice," Clarene responded. "We've all but ignored you on this trip. You've been so quiet. What is it?"

"I have the strangest feeling something on the other side of the lake is calling to me."

"You do? What's it saying?"

"I can't describe it, but it's kinda like a message is trying to get through. Something's going to happen here. I just know it. Something is telling me to be ready."

Clarene looked at her with a warm smile. "Does it have to do with Antonia-Maria?"

"I think so, but I'm not sure. The energy around this lake is so powerful and confusing to me. I want to relax with it, but I'm afraid of being drawn back into the drama and I sure don't want to experience that cave again!"

"Don't worry, Janice, that's not going to happen. As for the other, just let it come in its own way, at its own pace. You'll be ready for it, I'm sure."

Carl and his boat remained hidden from view. As night fell, the LASO chopper returned to the Los Robles Valley airport and it was replaced with a San Ramon Sheriff's helicopter called in by Rodriguez. It's powerful searchlight arced over and around the lake, causing much speculation on the ground amongst the tourists in their RVs, but no sign of the elusive rancher and his boat were seen.

"Well," Rodriguez asked Clarene, "what do you see in all this? Should we spend the night or come back in the morning?"

"I don't feel that McCormick will try to reach the dam before early morning," she replied. "When I say early morning, I mean in the dark just before dawn comes over the mountains. I think he will count on us being asleep, allowing him to slip in and out."

"What if you're wrong?"

"Then it doesn't hurt to leave a man or two down by the dam to keep watch. If he shows up before we return, they can radio you and then scare him off. He won't be very eager to drop drums in the water if they're around, and it will give us time to get here, so you can take him into custody."

"Well, you seem to have been right, so far. I know we all have to get some rest tonight, so it seems like a good plan…" Rodriguez suddenly cocked his ear towards his cruiser. "Hang on a second, lady. There's a message coming through on my radio."

He walked away from the group and then dropped his ear closer to the speaker/mike attached to the shoulder flap on his uniform shirt.

A moment later he walked back and said, "Your LASO buddies are back at the station and want to know if they should join us here. I told them to stay put; that we were calling it a night and that we'd join them for dinner shortly."

Clarene nodded and motioned to Victor and Janice to join her at the Sheriff's cruiser, parked nearby. Rodriguez had them back in Los Robles within a half-hour.

SEVENTEEN

Tuesday Morning

It was 'o'dark thirty,' as Bill was fond of saying, when they all met again at the Sheriff's station. Dressed for the crisp morning air, the two women and four men made ready to resume their pursuit of a madman trying to blow up the dam.

Nothing had been heard from the Deputies that had been assigned to stay at the lake during the night, so Clarene and the others knew that Carl had remained hidden. Tired and cold, the two were immediately sent home by Rodriguez as soon as he and the others arrived.

"Should we find a boat and start cruising the lake?" asked Bill. "Maybe we can flush him out."

"No, it's too early; there's no one up to rent one to us," Rodriguez replied. "Besides, we'd have most of the RVrs up trying to shoot us for waking them with all the noise. After that, they'd stay up and get in our way."

"Our best course," said Clarene, "is to wait near the dam. It'll be the same as when the deputies were in place. When he sees us, he won't be able to do anything but scramble to get away."

"Sounds good to me," Bill answered for them all, realizing

that while *they* wouldn't be making a lot of noise, Carl would have to make at least some, in trying to get the boat near the gates. "All we have to do is listen for the sound of those big outboards," he said, as he started walking. "Anyone know the way?"

"Yes," answered Rodriguez. "Just follow my lead."

With Rodriguez in front, the six of them formed a line of bodies in the near darkness, heading towards the rear of the dam and its huge gates. The light from a disappearing moon, reflecting through the clear air, gave enough radiance to guide their way.

Even this small a group had its pecking order, for behind Rodriguez was Bill's Captain, then Clarene and Victor, followed by Janice. Bill brought up the rear on purpose to be near her. In the rocky, rough areas, he reached out to steady her. Eventually he took her by the hand, walking in front of her, to lead.

At the point where the trail ended, Rodriguez opened a small duffel bag he was carrying and pulled out some powerful flashlights. He gave one each to Bill and his Captain and kept the last one for himself.

With no place to sit down, the group had no choice but to move around, smashing down the grasses and weeds as quietly as they could, to make room to stand more comfortably.

Now they waited.

* * *

Far up the lake, Carl awoke in the seat of the boat and stretched his aching muscles. He had pulled into a small cove around noon the day before and using brush and the limbs of the overhanging trees, had camouflaged himself quite well. He had seen the LASO helicopter roaming the area, but hadn't been concerned with its presence, but when the small chopper with the spotlight had started in the night, he knew they were looking for him.

Still, he stayed hidden, knowing that the morning would aid him, that people would be tired from looking for him all night, that they would be at their worst, making mistakes that would let him get through. From the time his plan had been conceived, he knew there was no stopping him from getting it done! He was a McCormick, he *would* succeed!

As the night had worn on, he had slept fitfully, constantly turning, seeking comfort on a small boat cushion designed to seat three.

He had been in the cove for almost sixteen hours and it was now time to began the final act of his revenge. Checking his surroundings one last time to ensure that no one could see him, he removed the dynamite from the large tool box he had placed by the driver's seat and began taping it into bundles before inserting it into the inner drums. After setting and hooking up the timers to the blasting caps taped within the bundles, he sealed the inner drums off. The dynamite was now waterproof.

The timers were set to explode at 5:30 a.m., plenty of time for him to get the boat down to the gates and lower the drums into place and then get away.

He looked at his luminous watch and saw that it was 4:30 a.m. It was time to go and, making sure no one was about, he cut the boat loose from its hiding place and quietly poled it out to the main part of the lake. The moon's fading light helped guide his way.

He had chosen the borrowed boat carefully, knowing that while it was used primarily for water skiing, the owner also used it for fishing in the larger Sierra lakes. As a result, his friend had added a small, electric trolling motor which was mounted through a watertight connection through the centerline of the hull. In such a position, it exerted maximum power and maneuverability without measurable noise or difficulty in operating. It was perfect for Carl's needs.

He turned the key and started the small motor and the boat immediately, but quietly and smoothly, picked up the needed speed, heading him for the docks and the dam beyond. It was still some time to dawn, but he knew it would soon begin inkling its way over the mountains toward him. He must be done by then.

The boat crept past the dock area and began its final bearing towards the gates of the dam. Its' dark color blended in well with the earth and trees of the surrounding area, making it and him almost invisible, as well as silent.

A short while later, he cut the electric motor and drifted quietly to a point close to the column that rose between the first two gates. The boat bumped to a stop against the concrete pillar.

Not twenty yards away Rodriguez heard the thump and quickly pointed his light's powerful beam at the spot he thought it had come from. Two more beams from the lights held by Bill and his Captain also pierced the darkness, converging at the same spot.

Carl was startled by the lights, but they were pointed at the next gate over, missing him by yards. Moments later, when nothing appeared in their beams, they went off.

Warned now that someone was there and that they were suspicious of sounds coming from the back of the dam, Carl took stock of the situation, trying to determine what to do.

The timers were set and time was running out. It would take him at least five to ten minutes to carefully roll the drums over the side of the boat and then guide them with the ropes to their resting-places by the columns. There was no way he could do that and avoid being heard, especially if there were people just waiting there, listening for suspicious noises.

He wondered what would happen if he just dumped the drums into the water near the gates and ran, hoping they might get close enough to the gates to be effective. The next second he dropped the thought as a bad idea.

It then occurred to him to sink the boat itself behind the

center gate, letting the full force of all three drums of explosives do their job on it alone. That seemed to offer the best opportunity for success, for once the boat was sunk, those on the shore couldn't do anything to prevent the drums from exploding.

Nodding his head to himself, he decided that's what he would do. But, then it dawned on him – how was he to sink the boat? He had no tools to cut through the hull.

He began to worry about being heard again and reached out to keep the boat from bumping into the column and making more noise. But, in doing so, he misjudged the distance and lost his balance. Trying to right himself in the fading darkness, he staggered awkwardly around the drums and suddenly found himself dangling over the side of the boat, feet and legs still inside, arms and head just inches above the water.

Startled with his predicament, he desperately grabbed at one of the drums to pull himself back from the edge. As he clumsily tried to regain his balance, his temper cut loose with a torrent of vulgar swearing, loudly proclaiming his presence to those on shore.

They responded with three beams of powerful light, converging on him, the boat, and its contents.

Turning around to face the source, he angrily jabbed his middle finger into the air at them. Then, as those on shore began yelling at him to stop, he turned the key on the dashboard and pushed the starter buttons for the two powerful outboards. Holding the steering wheel hard over to the left, he jammed the throttles full forward and lurched into the seat as the bow thrust its nose high in the air, seeking freedom from those on shore.

The powerful beams stayed glued to him, though. Over the throaty roar of the motors, he heard them yelling at him to STOP!

Amidst the uproar, a sudden thought came to him. He could just ram the boat into the rear of the center gate; that would sink it! The timers would still work and he could yet be successful.

He slowed the boat and made a turn back to the dam, then went again to full power as he sought to complete his mission.

The loud noises and the flashes from the shore were confusing to him at first, but as the angry zips of the bullets whizzed past his head and body, he realized he was being shot at. The resounding thuds and hollow echoes told him they had the range of the boat and he would be next.

Realizing they could and would stop him short of his goal, he decided to retreat and head back to the docks. He would be there well before them, and while they were worrying about defusing the bombs, he could get away.

The bullets kept coming, even after he turned away, but the range was increasing by the second. Two hit the back of the boat in succession and then, no more.

He turned the wheel to adjust his course, but there was no response. He turned it harder, moving it from full right to full left with no effect on his course. As the first glimmer of dawn edged its way towards the mountains, he found that he was heading at full speed towards the far shore, to a point just below the spot where that strange rock stood poised on the hillside. In desperation, he pulled the throttles back, but the boat failed to slow. Seconds later, it slammed and shuddered to a violent stop, the pointed nose of its bow thrust deeply into the mud of the wall of the lake.

The abrupt stop propelled him off the driver's seat, over the windshield. He was hurt. Both hands were sprained and he found it difficult to move his left leg. As he sat there contemplating his fate, he noticed the water coming into the boat from the bow. It was slowly, but surely sinking.

He tried to get up and get off, but there was nowhere to go, for the wall of mud was too slick and too high to climb. He knew the water on this side of the lake was shallower, but still too deep to walk in. He slumped back into the seat, dejected and defeated. Whatever time was left on the timers, was all he had left for himself. He wondered if there would be any pain.

On the far side of the shore, Rodriguez and the others could barely make out the boat. They weren't sure what Carl was doing, but they could see they had stopped him from reaching the dam. A few moments later, as the boat continued sinking, they realized the situation and called for Carl to answer. When he failed to respond, Rodriguez decided to commandeer a boat from the slips at the dock to see what his condition was.

Bill and his Captain joined him in running to the docks, and the three men were soon crossing the lake in a small motor boat. As they reached the middle of the lake they watched as Carl's impaled craft slowly slipped from view beneath the water. They saw no one get off.

"Get your lights on that area," Rodriguez ordered, pointing to where the speedboat had disappeared. Two beams thrust forward to illuminate the muddy wall, but the men saw nothing, save a patch of bubbles indicating where the boat had gone down.

"Do you see him?" Rodriguez asked. No matter what Carl had attempted, Rodriguez wanted to save him, if he could.

"No," Bill replied, straining to find any sign that Carl had survived.

"Well, we're going to keep looking, anyway," Rodriguez exclaimed. "I can't just let him disappear under the water without trying to find him. I owe that much to him, so does the city."

"Yeah," said Bill's Captain. "It's over now, let's wrap it up proper."

"Wait a minute!" Bill said, suddenly pulling on Rodriguez's shoulder. "What about the explosives? Weren't they set on timers?"

Rodriguez looked at Bill and immediately pulled the throttle, slowing the boat to a crawl. "Yeah. That's what Victor told us he saw back in the barn. What time do you think they would be set for?"

"Clarene said the explosions in her dream went off just at dawn, and the sun is just now coming up. I don't think there's much time left, do yo...?"

The dangling question was brazenly interrupted by three mighty explosions erupting through the surface of the lake. A tremendous force of water gushed high unto the muddy walls and then, pulled by overwhelming gravity, cascaded back, cleansing and clearing the walls down to their rocky substructure. At the same time, a huge wave hurled outward towards the three men and their boat, ready to inundate them and anything else in its way.

They could only grab the sides of their little boat in terror and desperation as the wave and the smaller sisters it spawned, pulsed and pounded around and past them. The boat was repeatedly thrown and twisted about before it finally ended.

The sun was coming up well over the mountains when they regained control and pointed their boat once more towards the far shore.

They soon saw large patches of debris rising to the surface, where it waited to be recovered, or blown away by the morning breeze. The closer they got to where Carl's boat had gone down, the more they saw. Small pieces of cloth and wood were intermixed with large pieces of molded plastic. Identifiable boat parts floated on the surface, as if they were waiting to be rejoined with other floating parts to become whole again.

As they moved through the debris, Bill saw two strange objects suspended and twisting slowly just under the surface of the water. Using his hand as a paddle, he brought the boat closer. One of the objects appeared to be entangled in a large piece of cloth that seemed to keep it from sinking. Paddling the boat even closer, he reached into the water and pulled the object to the surface.

When he got it up, he could see that it was a skull, probably that of a man. After untangling the cloth, he passed it over to the two Captains. As they examined it, Bill reached into the water again and pulled up the other object, this one small and spindly, like the remains of a woman's hand. It too, was entangled in some cloth, which was covered with small clods of mud. Quickly removing the encrusted mud away, he discovered a small ring around one of the fingers. He looked at it for a few seconds, then cautiously watching to see that he wasn't observed by the others, removed it and placed it in his pocket.

"What is that?" asked Rodriguez. Bill jerked around with a startled look on his face, sure that he had been caught, but Rodriguez was only looking at the bony hand he was holding.

"That can't be part of McCormick," Rodriguez exclaimed. "The blast would have torn him apart, but not like *that*. The flesh is all gone. Those have to be old bones, just like this is an old skull" he said, hoisting it. This stuff has been down there for a long time."

"About two hundred years, I'd say," Bill replied.

"How do you know that?" Rodriguez was incredulous at the pompous assumption of this fella from L.A.

"It's kinda an involved story, Captain, and I think it would be better coming from Clarene or Victor. I know Clarene shared a lot with you about why she got involved with tracking down Carl in the first place. But, there's another story she hasn't told you about, yet. In fact, if you look at it a certain way, it's a case you just helped close."

Sheriff Rodriguez nodded his head, slowly, quizzically. He didn't know what this fella Edwards was referring to, but he could always use credit for solving a case; especially if the credit was being given to him by an expert from LASO.

* * *

Back on shore, Clarene stood with the others in the parking lot and offered a short version of Janice's life as Antonia-Maria to Rodriguez. Rodriguez was interested, but skeptical. While he had been developing a growing enchantment with Clarene's abilities, he wasn't prepared to accept the past lives drama merely on her say-so. No indeed, he needed something substantial to convince him about this!

Turning to Bill's boss he said jokingly, "Do you have to personally deal with her, or do you leave that to Deputy Edwards?"

"I leave most of it to Deputy Edwards, but there have been times when I've had the pleasure of a one-on-one session."

"Really? So have I, Captain…Captain…?" Rodriguez stopped, cocked his head a bit with a puzzled look on his face and asked, "Just what the hell is your name, anyway? We got introduced in such a hurry back at the station, I didn't get it."

"It's Hendersen. Jack Hendersen."

"Nice to meet you, Jack," he said, reaching out to shake his hand. "It's been a real pleasure doing business with you. But, I know you'll understand when I tell you, I don't ever want to work with you like this, again!"

They all laughed.

Rodriguez turned back to Clarene and said, "Getting back to Janice being Antonia-Maria in a past life, how do you prove such a story? How do you ever know for sure that Antonia-Maria has come back to us now as Janice?"

Clarene started to respond, but Bill held his left hand up to stop her, at the same time reaching into his pocket with the other. "I don't think," he said, "you could ever prove the story to everyone's satisfaction, but maybe this will help." He held out his hand to Janice, fist turned up and closed around the ring.

"What is it?" she asked, curiously.

"The explosions churned up some old things from way below the surface and we found this floating amongst the debris," he said, opening his fist to reveal the gold band laying in his palm. "I think you'll find it very interesting. It seems to be about two hundred years old."

"How do you know that?" she asked, gingerly taking the ring.

"From the date engraved inside."

"Date?" she said, squinting at the inside of the ring. "I don't see a date."

"Here," he said, holding out his hand again, "use this little magnifying glass I keep on my keychain. I had to use it myself, since the date is so small."

Janice took the little glass and focused on the inside of the band, then gasped.

"Oh, my god!" she cried out as the ring and the glass dropped from her hand and tumbled to the asphalt near Victor. Clarene quickly put her arms around her shoulders as Janice started to shake and sob.

Victor picked up the ring and the magnifying glass to look for himself. "I see the date," he said peering intently, "I think it's 1826. And, there's some initials here, too. There's an 'A,'...an 'M,'...and a 'G.'" He stopped for a moment, slowly shaking his head from side to side in complete amazement.

"Good God!" he exclaimed after a moment, "this must have belonged to Antonia-Maria! I bet her father gave it to her when she left on the coach for San Ramon!"

Janice turned towards him and with an unsteady hand, reached out to retrieve the ring. She gently kissed it before grasping it tightly in her left hand. Tears welled up in her eyes as she quietly said her thanks to Bill, then turned back to being held again by Clarene.

The group turned quiet, each of them deep in their own thoughts with the story of Antonia-Maria running through their minds.

Victor finally broke the silence. Nervously fingering the bald spot at the back of his head, he asked hesitantly, "Did you find anything else?"

"Like...what?" Bill responded cautiously, full of concern that somehow Victor had overheard their conversation in the boat about the skull and the bony remains of the hand. He certainly didn't want to bring that up now.

"Well, you know...," Victor flustered with the words, not wanting to appear tactless, or obsessed with the matter, "...like anything that could prove that the gold, or the silver map are still down there."

"Nothing," said Bill, watching for a reaction on Rodriguez's face. "Nothing like what you're looking for, I'm afraid. Nothing like that, at all."

"That's right," Rodriguez added. "But, if anyone wants to come back and look on their own," he said softly, "you never can tell, I just might help them. I *do* have the resources, you know."